The Sandlot Legacy

CHRONICLES OF YOUTH AND BASEBALL

WALTER A. BEEDE

© Copyright 2023 - All rights reserved.

The content contained within this book may not be reproduced, duplicated, or transmitted without direct written permission from the author or the publisher.

Under no circumstances will any blame or legal responsibility be held against the publisher, or author, for any damages, reparation, or monetary loss due to the information contained within this book, either directly or indirectly.

Legal Notice:

This book is copyright protected. It is only for personal use. You cannot amend, distribute, sell, use, quote, or paraphrase any part or the content within this book, without the consent of the author or publisher.

Disclaimer Notice

Please note the information contained within this document is for educational and entertainment purposes only. All effort has been executed to present accurate, up-to-date, reliable, and complete information. No warranties of any kind are declared or implied. Readers acknowledge that the author is not engaged in the rendering of legal, financial, medical, or professional advice. The content within this book has been derived from various sources. Please consult a licensed professional before attempting any techniques outlined in this book.

By reading this document, the reader agrees that under no circumstances is the author responsible for any losses, direct or indirect, that are incurred because of the use of the information contained within this document, including, but not limited to, errors, omissions, or inaccuracies.

Table of Contents

CHAPTER 1 5
    Dreams of the Sandlot 6

CHAPTER 2 19
    The Mysterious Mentor 20

CHAPTER 3 37
    The Big Game 38

CHAPTER 4 55
    A New Challenge 56

CHAPTER 5 65
    A Chance Encounter 66

CHAPTER 6 75
    A Mentor's Wisdom 76

CHAPTER 7 _____ 81
Dreams Take Flight _____ 82

CHAPTER 8 _____ 111
Stepping onto New Grounds _____ 112

CHAPTER 9 _____ 121
The Journey to the Majors _____ 122

CHAPTER 10 _____ 133
The Rookie Season _____ 134

CHAPTER 11 _____ 145
All-Star Aspirations _____ 146

CHAPTER 12 _____ 155
Legacy and Lessons _____ 156

CHAPTER 13 _____ 163
Memories and Reminiscences _____ 164

Prologue

In the vast tapestry of life, dreams are the vibrant threads that weave stories of ambition and determination. Jack Thompson's journey is emblematic of every child who gazes at the stars and believes in the power of their own aspirations. Dreams are not the idle musings of the mind; they are the pulse of potential, the songs of our soul beckoning us toward greatness.

Yet, for every dreamer, there stands a chorus of skeptics. Like shadows, they cling to us, casting doubts and emphasizing our limitations. But herein lies the paradox of dreams: they aren't born from abundance but from the tenacity of spirit. Jack's tale is a testament to the heart's resilience, echoing that real courage isn't just about chasing dreams but doing so when the entire world expects you to falter.

Spanish poet Juan Goytisolo's poignant words from the 1980s capture the essence of this journey: "Life is beautiful, you will see..." Through Jack's story, we are gently reminded that amid life's trials, a beacon of hope, love, and camaraderie always emerges.

And just as dreamers possess a unique energy, they also hold the magic of transformation. Their unwavering belief is a potent force capable of reigniting dormant dreams in others. While they grapple with doubt, as we all do, they never let it snuff out their light. Instead, their luminescence draws others towards them, illuminating pathways previously unseen.

But dreams aren't gifts bestowed upon the select few. They are challenges, laying down the gauntlet for those brave enough to pick it up. They don't discriminate between victories and losses; they focus on the journey. As Jack discovers, joy doesn't solely reside in the destination but flourishes in pursuing one's passion.

Yet, what is life if not a series of unpredictable twists? When darkness looms, life often surprises us with moments of serendipity. These gifts may come through friendships, chance encounters, or personal revelations. They are the universe's gentle nudges, reminding us to persevere and find beauty in the unexpected.

Central to this narrative is the power of human connection. Just as Jack's trajectory is forever altered by George Davis's mentorship, so are our lives shaped by the influences around us. These relationships - with friends, mentors, or family - sculpt our reality and infuse our futures with potential.

But while Jack's story may read like a tale of baseball and ambition, it is, at its core, a celebration of kindness and influence. It serves as a reminder that our everyday gestures, however small, can transform lives.

This narrative is not just about dreams realized but also about gratitude - a recognition that the beauty of life lies in its details. Our true legacy is what we achieve, the memories we leave in people's hearts, and the smiles we bring to their faces.

Prologue

As we embark on Jack's journey, remember: every road is a canvas yet to be painted. The beauty isn't just in reaching the horizon but in the tales, we weave along the way. Dream, persevere, and let your story shine.

CHAPTER 1

Dreams of the Sandlot

I was just a child back then.

When I reached twelve, my world revolved around an idyllic haven known as Willow Creek. A sleepy town cradled in the embrace of Northern California; this magical place possessed an ethereal charm that whispered through its sun-kissed summers. The clear waters of the Trinity River, a majestic ribbon of liquid sapphire, wove its way through the landscape, glistening with tranquility and peace that bordered on enchantment. In this corner of paradise, time meandered lazily as if reluctant to disrupt the rhythm of a perfectly imperfect life.

The air was crisp, cleansed by twenty million trees, and sweetened by a billion lilies, irises, and black-eyed Susan's scattered across the landscape. It tasted sweet as if nature had added extra sugar to the recipe. Willow Creek was a cocoon of solace, nurturing kids like me with a sense of serenity. It was a realm where simplicity reigned supreme, where the embrace of family mixed with community transcended the bounds of ordinary connection.

It was an ideal place to grow up — calm, quiet, and safe. Strangers were transformed into family the first time you met them.

But there were few strangers in Willow Creek, a town so small everyone had a story to tell about where their family was and what their family was doing on the day they were born or the time their uncle helped them fix the fencing on the hog pen. It was a familiarity as warm as a blanket on an icy winter morning. Their smiles, etched with the memories of countless shared moments, adorned their countenances like precious relics. In the embrace of Willow Creek, I was not merely a face in the crowd but an integral part of its unique tapestry. I didn't know then, but that acquaintance, that kindness in people, was what a kid like me needed. Somebody who trusted that, against all odds, I could become the man who now tells this story.

Nestled in the heart of Willow Creek was a sanctuary that made magic palpable. Here, amidst the whispers of old trees, was a place that held the very soul of Willow Creek — a sandlot. This was no pristine field with chalk-lined bases, but a makeshift baseball realm that revealed its history in every divot and patch. The diamond was discreetly hidden behind a series of venerable oaks, but its significance was anything but secret. Every base had been crafted with care; old white T-shirts, sewn up and filled with the very sand that made this lot so iconic, marked the critical points of the field. The earth below was a testament to the care and commitment of its young athletes: patches of grass interspersed with areas of dirt, with fewer rocks now than in springs past, thanks to the diligent hands of neighborhood kids who made it a ritual to clear them away before the season's games commenced.

There were no man-made barriers here, no fences to cordon off the area. Instead, nature itself played a part in the game. A massive oak tree stood sentinel in centerfield, its branches stretching wide, marking over 350 feet. Behind the big oak tree where a set of railroad tracks that several times a day had railroad cars carrying coal north to the pacific northwest. A ball hit there was the stuff of legends, a testament to a player's prowess.

Baseball, in our town, was so much more than just another game. It was our bond, our rite of passage. It was the medium through which we cultivated friendships, brewed healthy rivalries, and connected with a legacy greater than ourselves. That sandlot, that sacred ground, was where children stopped being mere dreamers and transformed into the baseball titans they revered. For a few golden hours, the shadows of McCovey, Marichal, and Mays would dance alongside us, inspiring our movements. But when it was time for action, time for the bat to meet the ball, the only echoes that mattered were those of our own names, cheered on by our imaginary, yet ever-present, throngs of fans.

There and only there, imagination and reality switched places, and we became anything our minds could conceive.

I was just a normal kid with a slight build and unruly brown hair that dangled between my eyes every time I whipped my head to catch a fly ball or hit a pitch into the outfield. I don't know why I never cut it. Perhaps it was because of my father. While other fathers scolded their sons for the length of their hair, mine liked to ruffle my hair as a greeting. I always complained when he did, but I secretly loved it. It was one of the many things that was just his and mine alone.

"Dad," I whined.

"One more for good luck," he laughed, tousling my waiting head again.

My dad had never played baseball growing up in Italy. Our national pastime was just a passing fancy on the other side of the world. They treated soccer - which they called *football* - with all the same passion and reverence, but my dad had never been much of an athlete. He had started working from a young age to help his own family, and that was his focus here as well.

He used to say I had mischievous eyes — curious eyes that revealed the funny ideas in my head. I was always careful to let people see my happier side, confident they would not enjoy the alternative: the gaze that spoke of the hidden sadness that sometimes overwhelmed me. No, I preferred to offer the world a more straightforward side of myself, just a normal kid with brown hair and plain blue eyes. How could I be anything but happy in a life that seemed perfect to anyone looking from the outside in? It was my duty to uphold the illusion of a cheerful youth.

I loved my parents with all my heart, but mine was still somewhat of a lonely life. They worked tirelessly at jobs that kept a roof over our heads and food at our table, but just barely. Being immigrants didn't usually add up to high-paying jobs, so they took on every opportunity they could, no matter how little it paid or how grueling it seemed. They were gone for long hours and sometimes at night as well. The fact that I was an only child as well made it lonely and quiet at times for long stretches at home. I knew they were doing everything to provide for me and help me access a better future, but plenty of times I think I would have traded that uncertain future for more time as a family in the present.

But my face lit up and any lingering doubts fell off my face the first time I stumbled upon the sandlot. It was like finding hidden treasure, tucked back off the roads where no one could see it if they didn't know what to look for. My first day there I had been laughing with a friend as we ran after a rabbit that we had accidentally flushed while racing through the woods near my house. We lost track of the rabbit but eventually heard the unmistakable sounds of kids laughing and having a good time, and there was an instant pull for me to see what it was all about and see if there was a place for me among them. While baseball eventually became the greatest passion of my life, the real lure at first was that sound of perfect happiness, of the kind of second family that I hadn't realized I had been looking for.

Like most kids in Willow Creek, I was far from a natural athlete. Gangly, with long, thin arms that went their own way and clumsy coordination, it was ten times harder for me to throw or catch a ball. It's no wonder I was often overlooked and undervalued as a player by my peers. Still, I always dreamt of being an integral part of a team and making a play that earned the respect of my friends. It didn't take long to learn that my baseball skills were neither good nor good enough.

Sometimes kids can be ruthless, and I found myself on the sidelines more times than I can count. That, and always being the last one to be picked for a game, were constant reminders that I was different from the other kids who zipped around the bases, slid into home plate, and won the accolades of the close-knit band. I still remember the pounding in my chest when I showed up to play. But I kept showing up, hopeful that something would eventually click and make me an expert at the game I loved. Hoping against hope that the doubts that were shouted at me daily to quit were premature. Day after day, I fought the notion that the dream I was clinging to was slipping through my fingers.

I could just imagine the conversations at the town diner:

"Did you see the kids play yesterday, Chester?"

"Sure did. That was a good one. And did you see how Tommy was throwing that baseball?"

"Couldn't miss it if I was blind in one eye and couldn't see out the other. I tell you what: that boy is destined for the Majors!"

"He sure is. But that Thompson boy. My word. The kid is all hat and no cattle."

"Don't I know it! He's about as useful as a screen door on a submarine."

To be fair, I never heard a negative word from anyone. But it wasn't hard to convince myself that those words were being uttered. Thankfully, I learned at an incredibly early age not to be discouraged. I had seen my family hold it together after every problem in our way. Storm after storm, crisis after crisis, my family remained resolute. I had learned it by osmosis as much as by teaching, so there was no chance I would give up. After every game, long after the other kids had gone home or been treated to ice cream for their solid gameplay, I stayed in that lot — sometimes for hours. I practiced by throwing balls high, squinting into the sun, and running back to catch them. I missed more than I could catch, but that never stopped me. I practiced until the sun dipped over the mountains, and I was muddy with sweat and dust. Running, catching, sliding — I tried to make my awkward limbs match the images that played in my mind of the players in the Majors and the stars of my sandlot.

I spent hundreds of hours at the sandlot, with my weathered glove and scuffed baseball cap always by my side. When the other kids didn't let me play in the game, I studied — laser-focused on their movements, actions, and decisions. Later, on my way home, I would stop by the library and check out as many books as I could about baseball legends. I devoured the information inside, determined to learn as much about the mental game as I could. My family wasn't home at night, but for a while that was OK. Because I was having dinner with Joe DiMaggio, Ted Williams, Lou Gehrig, Cy Young, and Babe Ruth. I memorized Gehrig's speech about being the luckiest man on the face of the Earth.

I read how Ted Williams had missed five seasons of his prime fighting in World War II and Korea. I marveled at DiMaggio, who before he was the Yankee Clipper, had been a San Francisco Seal and once hit in 61 straight games. And when I was sure no one was looking, I pretended to be them. I accepted the MVP award, bowing humbly to the Commissioner and waving to my adoring fans.

I let the roar of the crowd blow through my hair. I even winked at the pretty girls who leaned over the dugout just to touch my hand. I dreamed bigger than I could ever afford as I listened to the sound of my name over the loudspeaker shouted loud by the honey-throated announcer as I was introduced to the field:

"And now, Ladies and Gentlemen, please direct your attention to the baseline as we welcome the starting lineup. Number 11, leading off, the Center Fielder, Jack…"

The thunderous resound of the crowd would sweep through the air, engulfing everything in its mighty roar. Its sheer intensity was so overpowering that the rest of my name might as well have been a fragile whisper, so consumed and lost within the rising cacophony.

I would trot out onto the field, humbly receiving the praise of the fans, confident that I was the anchor of the team. Children would wave cards bearing my picture, longing for my signature. Men in jeans and women in skirts would scream my name when my headfirst burst out of the dugout. They were grown-ups with houses and jobs and bills to pay, but when they saw me in real life, they were kids again, rooting for their heroes.

Like I said, I was just a kid back then. I didn't know what really mattered in life. I didn't understand what lay behind the screaming crowds. I couldn't respect the work, discipline, physical pain, and mental endurance players developed. I had big dreams... and that was enough. On those solitary afternoons, alone in the sandlot, I did the things I wished I could do when all of Willow Creek flooded the grandstand. I stood tall in the batter's box, swinging with gusto and recoiling momentarily at the crack of the wood as it smacked the ball and sent it flying, imagining the faces of my friends the day I would finally manage to hit a home run, the cheers and applause in the distance as I tapped every single base; the rush from their admiration for my hard work; the pride of finally knowing that I was one of them.

As the summer days stretched on, the children of Willow Creek converged on the sandlot. We didn't seem to be weighed down with that mixture of frustration and hope as I was. Carefree, we took to the field with laughter. In short order, the sound of the crack of the bat echoed through the air like a symphony. It would be years before I knew we were a motley crew of young souls, each with their own sadness, frustrations, dreams, fears, and quirks.

The pack leader, Tommy, wore broad shoulders and an easy smile under a mop of blonde ringlets. He was always ready to rally the team and remind them they were all together. Beside him, sweet Susie, with her fire engine hair and freckled face, offered a steady supply of humor and wit that could make even the toughest kids laugh. The last guy to stammer something about girls not being able to play with boys had taken her fastball between the shoulder blades when he came to bat, and never said another word about it.

And then there was Billy, the quiet dark-haired one, who hid behind thick glasses and always seemed to know just what to say to lift the spirits of his friends when the game wasn't going their way. These kids were the heart of the sandlot, and even though I was often left on the outskirts, I couldn't help but feel part of the team anyway. Still, I knew there was a deeper connection to be had. When I saw them playing, they were a family, bonded by their shared love for baseball, memories of games they shared, and the unspoken promise that they would always be there for each other no matter what happened on the field.

I really wanted to be part of that family. To be friends with Tommy, laugh with Susie, and let my heart be warmed up by Billy. Indeed, there was a place for me; but I couldn't find it.

I never figured out my unique contribution to the stew that was our team. So, I sat on the bench or stood along the chain-linked fence, waiting, hoping, wanting. I was too young to understand that dreams are only those — dreams. They are the mind's way of offering a preview of something great that is to come. And I might have missed my chance had it not been for my parents' lessons in perseverance. I might have been lanky and uncoordinated, today, but I also didn't understand the meaning of giving up and was willing to work day in and day out, past the point of exhaustion and pushing the limits of his endurance just for a shot.

During that summer, nobody believed I could make a big play in a real game. But I was determined to prove them all wrong. From the bottom of my heart, I was a player waiting to be seen; like a caterpillar trapped in a chrysalis, something was growing that had never been before. Every effort I poured into my growth as a player was worth it — for the pure love of the game and, of course, so that the other kids could see it. Without fail, I would arrive early to every game while the sand was pristine and undisturbed to practice my swings, field my ground balls, and run laps around the bases until my legs ached. My lungs burned, but it was a glorious flame within me as I imagined I could defeat that imaginary adversary. Then, after the game, I watched the bleachers empty, and cars drive away from the parking lot. Then, when I was sure they couldn't see me, I did it all again. The sacrifices of a hopeful determined to win that one game.

Every step was a celebration of my determination. Then, one day, something clicked inside me. Although I was still not good enough, I could not deny that something shifted and locked into place. That made me work even harder until one day, one of the happiest of my life, the ball went where I sent it. My legs aligned and moved me where I wanted to go. The other kids started to notice the changes in me as well. It was a simple thing, really. The sort of play you see is made three times a game if you're watching the Major Leaguers on TV. When we didn't have a game for a few days, they'd let me onto the field to shag fly balls or play first base so the rest could practice their throws across the diamond. We didn't use a scoreboard or umpires or coaches, but we all learned to keep all that information in our heads as the game went on.

There was one out and we were in the field, with me manning first. Billy was at the plate and Tommy was on the mound. Tommy threw a pitch that didn't break right, and Billy swung as hard as he could, smashing it down the first-base line toward the right-field corner. It was an easy double and the runner on first, Davey Winder, took off at the crack of the bat, determined to round the bases and score from first.

Except… none of that happened.

I'll be the first to admit that I flung my glove up largely in self-defense as Billy crushed the wayward fastball. But even in that moment of self-preservation, my slowly learned skills born of thousands of repetitions kicked in.

WHUMP!

The most beautiful sound in the world when you're in the field. The sound of leather absorbing the force of a baseball. I had caught Billy's surefire double for an out. After two seconds of wide-eyed staring, I remembered the situation and took two quick steps to touch first base with my foot. Davey was already around second base, clueless to what had happened. If there had been an official scorer on hand, the notation would have read DP 3-U: an unassisted double play executed by yours truly.

Billy's mouth fell open in sheer disbelief. He didn't stop as much as his legs just stopped responding to commands from his brain. Tommy gave a whooping cheer and ran to me, patting me on the back repeatedly and hollering, "Atta boy, Jack! Atta boy!"

But it was Susie who really touched me that day. She was always cracking jokes and keeping everyone on their toes with their quips and harmless insults. As I jogged past her, a huge grin still on my face, she touched my arm lightly and said, "I knew you could do it, Jack." At that moment, if she had asked me to strike out Mickey Mantle, I think I could have done it in three pitches.

Today, I look back and laugh at my need for those other kids' approval and gaining newfound respect among my peers. Years later, I can feel the pride and relief of no longer being the punchline to their jokes or the last one picked. I gained something more significant than that. I learned to love that kid. It was that kid who put in the work, endured the pain, and earned friends for life. That kid, little Jack Thompson, proved that, although he was not the best, he was no longer the worst.

I was just a kid back then, living my 12-year-old life. But it was that version of me who won the game of his life by learning that you don't have to be the best; you just have to give the best effort to get the payoff and that when you love something as much as I have always loved and will always love baseball, everything you sacrifice will pale in comparison to what you will receive in return.

Just like the meandering roads that wind through the picturesque landscapes and ascend the rolling hills of Northern California, life frequently opts for the scenic route to lead us toward our dreams and destiny. Along this path, we encounter hurdles, obstacles, and unexpected detours that test our resolve. We have a choice in how we respond: we can bemoan the journey's challenges, allowing frustration to overshadow the beauty around us, or we can embrace the scenery that unfolds before our eyes, finding joy in the moments that make the expedition worthwhile. Life's scenic route invites us to appreciate the journey as much as the destination, to savor each twist and turn, and to discover wonders along the way. The greatest of these wonders is the power of unwavering determination and love for the game or whatever you love. With that as your foundation, there is no limit to how far you will go.

CHAPTER 2

The Mysterious Mentor

"Come on, Jack. We're going down to the sandlot. Can you play?"

The sound of my friends' knocks on the door each day that year filled me with joy. It was the summer I became a valued member of my team — the summer that changed my life forever. I remember the sensation of confidence growing inside me. With each game, the glove and the bat felt more like an extension of my body than a tool. The growing respect of the other kids was a fire crackling in my chest. Those once-sad eyes were now focused with determination to keep improving. I knew I had a long road before me, but I was happy to know my direction had shifted and I was going down the right path. After the fateful day of the unassisted double play, the older kids had kept me at first for a while. But as my legs got longer and I started to cover more ground on the basepaths, they decided my potential was wasted standing motionless for most plays. One day, Tommy asked me if I wanted to give it a go in center field, and I swelled with pride. All my reading had told me that a good manager puts his best defenders right up the middle of the field - catcher, shortstop, second base, and centerfield. They weren't looking for a place on the field to stick me, but rather somewhere to use my emerging talents. The summer memories were etched deep within my mind: every chuckle shared, every prank played, and every triumphant yell as someone raced to a makeshift base. Yet, one particular afternoon stands alone in the gallery of those cherished recollections. Alone on the sandlot, I was absorbed in refining my pitches, when an unfamiliar figure caught my eye. An elderly gentleman sat on the well-worn wooden bench, close enough to observe the field but far enough to not intrude. His presence was new to me, but the gentle aura he exuded made me believe he was no stranger to the dance of baseball. Maybe it was the way he sat, leaning in slightly whenever I pitched, or the sparkle in his eyes that revealed countless memories of games gone by.

Despite the comforting warmth I felt from him, his focused attention on my every move did stir a mix of curiosity and unease in me. The bench could have been full of spectators, but his gaze felt like he was only watching me. Was he a grandparent of one of the kids, I pondered, or perhaps an old fan reliving his memories of the game?

Trying to feign indifference initially, I continued to practice. But his reactions — a soft clap when I would catch my self-thrown popup, a sympathetic shake of his head when I missed — made it impossible to ignore his presence. Gathering all the courage my young self could muster, I decided to bridge the gap between us.

With a quick exhale, I approached him, my glove swinging gently by my side. "Excuse me, sir," my voice emerged more confidently than I felt, "I noticed you've been watching me. I'm working hard to improve my game. If you have any advice, I'd really appreciate it."

For a moment, he simply observed me, under his old worn-out Cleveland Indians hat, his ocean-blue eyes reflecting wisdom and understanding. It felt like an eternity before he responded, but when he did, it was with an infectious chuckle, one that seemed to echo stories of countless games and players of yesteryears. At that moment I felt that this man somehow knew more than he was letting on. While I did not know who he was, others around the sandlot seemed to know him and seemed to go out of their way to say hello to this older gentleman. At that moment, he was just a kind elder, enchanted by the same love for baseball that fueled my every pitch. Our paths had crossed on that sandlot, and from then on, the game would never be the same for either of us.

My boldness vanished instantly, leaving me with the same feeling of being nothing more than the joke I had worked so hard to escape.

But he stopped laughing as quickly as he started. It was because I looked like my soul was leaving my body. Later I would learn that his explosion of laughter was in admiration of me. He found my boldness and positive attitude amusing and endearing, so full of strength but also with a dash of indecision.

"Well, young man," he began with a deep voice roughened by age. "I might be able to teach you a thing or two about baseball, you know?" And he started laughing again as if there was an inside joke that only he understood.

I remember thinking it odd that the old man laughed a lot because, at that moment in my life, the passing of the years caused people to lose the ability to have fun. But, as I have been reminded, I was just a kid.

"My name is George," the man said, extending a large, wrinkled hand. "And you are…?"

"I'm Jack Thompson, sir. Nice to meet you."

"Nice to meet you too, young man. So, whatcha wanna know?"

A hundred questions passed through my mind. I considered rattling off a half-dozen to get this kind man to start talking. Then I decided to tell him the truth:

"Everything, sir. Just everything."

Over the next few weeks, George took me under his wing, sharing his knowledge and tutoring the young boy I was in the game's finer points. He showed me how to improve my grip on the bat, how to read the pitcher's signals, and the importance of footwork when fielding a ball. My sacred times before and after the game where I practiced alone were replaced with hours and hours together with George Davis on the sandlot, sharing our passion for baseball and forging a bond that transcended age, experience, and now, also time.

George always seemed to know more than he showed. He always behaved like he had a secret, and I was expected to follow the clues to unearth the treasure. And, oh, the treasures he had in store for me.

He seemed to enjoy teaching me, evidenced by his proud smile every time I did something right for the first time. He laughed if I got angry when I could not do a particular maneuver. But he never lost his patience in the many summers we were together.

That old man was with me every afternoon, talking to me about the details of good baseball and unearthing secrets of the field. For the first time, I knew what it was like to feel that I was important to someone, that I mattered. That I was worthy of somebody spending time with me.

My parents loved me. But their busy schedules always tempered their ability to express that love.

Sharing time with them was almost impossible. Weekdays were filled with earning a living to support our family, and weekends were reserved for the thousands of things they couldn't do during the week. Inside me, I knew that without their effort and hard work, we couldn't survive. But I couldn't get the ever-present feeling of missing and wanting more of them. We could have lived simply and pulled our belts a little tighter so they could work less. At least, then, I would have seen and enjoyed them. It would have been my father out on that dusty field, sweating beneath the California sun, teaching me how to play. I'd be lying if I hadn't wished a few times late at night that George was my real father, despite the obvious age difference. I love my dad with every fiber of my being, but George was providing the memories, the knowledge, and the praise that I never realized how badly I had hungered for from my dad.

Instead, it was George, this volunteer angel from another realm who sacrificed his time to teach me everything I know about baseball. Under his watchful eye, my skills improved rapidly. My throws grew stronger, my batting more consistent, and even my instincts on the field sharpened.

Occasionally, George would stick around and watch us practice, but mostly he just spent time with me. I didn't immediately tell my parents about him either. In fact, there were a few days when I was wondering if he really was a guardian angel. He seemed to appear out of nowhere, I never saw him anywhere else around town, and he didn't seem to have much interest in anyone else besides me when it came to coaching.

My years as an observer continued after I left the bench and joined the team on the field. I continued to study the other kids.

Only now, the other kids were looking at me, too, noticing my steady but sure transformation. Their whispers of incredulity and admiration.

"Good game, Jack," Susie said. "What, did you find some magic beans and climb a beanstalk?"

"Yeah, Jack. I mean, the way you stole third in the fourth inning. Nobody saw that comin'! Nobody! You got more nerve than a long-tailed cat in a room full of rocking chairs."

"Everybody is talking about it," Billy said. "I'm really happy for you. Keep up the good work."

Good work: Bill had no idea how true that was. It was hard work, long work, intense work. It was mental work and physical work. I limped home with a smile after every session with George, my brain moving quickly as my legs had. That was because George was teaching me the mental side of the game.

"Baseball is as much a game of the mind as it is of the body, young man," he would often say. He said it so often that, years later, I can sometimes still hear him, just as clearly as if I was back there with him by my side on that sandlot.

I couldn't see it then, but it was much more than the physical abilities that George helped me develop. He taught me the importance of mental strength and perseverance. He taught me to focus, discipline myself, and display a never-give-up attitude that I soon polarized into every aspect of my life. That summer, I wasn't aware that what I learned in baseball would define my whole life after.

One afternoon, he worked me out for two hours straight and could see that fatigue was creeping in. I struggled more and more to catch my breath completely.

"Let's take a break."

I dropped to the ground like a sack of potatoes, thrilled to have time to rest and regroup. But George didn't believe in rest. Even if your limbs needed a break, your brain was still on duty.

"So, who do you like to watch play, young man?"

I started rattling off a list of players I admired.

"Did you know that there was a major league player with the same name as you: George Davis? Maybe you like baseball so much because you share his passion and name, don't you think?" He laughed so hard that the birds pecking at worms in the nearby grass got spooked and flew away.

"Maybe. I've read about him."

"He was amazing. I'll bet you know a lot of famous players," I said dreamily. "I'll bet even you saw George Davis play."

"Hmmm," he chuckled, neither confirming nor denying.

"Why are you laughing, sir? It's true! George Davis played as a shortstop in the big leagues. It was long ago, but you must remember seeing him play!"

"Now, why would I know George Davis? How old do you think I am? 100?" That comment sent him into a fit of laughter that lasted longer than a minute, his rosy cheeks spreading their redness all over his face and down his neck.

I had always thought he laughed too much for an old man, but he couldn't stop that day. As I got angrier, his laughter increased, as if what I told him was the best of jokes. Back then, I felt infuriated; today, I still laugh at myself because of my 12-year-old innocence. I finally mustered the courage to ask.

"Sir, what is so funny? Why are you laughing?'

"I am George Davis, young man."

"I know your name, sir. I'm just saying that there is another George Davis who happened to be a major league baseball player and…" The moment's reality slowly washed over me like a wave on the Pacific Ocean.

"You don't hear me, young man. I am that George Davis."

Looking back, I think of this moment as one of the funniest days of my life; at the same time, it was one of the most embarrassing. I had spent hours and hours with a former major league baseball player and never realized it. But how could I? More than once, I remember thinking, "This old guy is playing a joke on me; how could he be an old baseball star?" The man next to me couldn't have ever been a young superstar. This man was born a senior citizen and remained so for his whole life. And a major league ball player? It didn't seem possible. How could someone with such a peculiar gait and appearance have been such a big shot in sports? Besides, in the few pictures I had seen of him, he was always serious, as if whatever was taking place in his thoughts was more important than what was happening in the world. How could this laughing old jokester in front of, and the somber-faced player be the same person?

"Don't play jokes on me, Mr. Davis! Are you serious?" I shot up from the ground and started pacing like a lion."

"Calm down, young man. You're sweatin' like a sinner in church."

"I'm sorry, sir. I don't mean to be rude. But you should have told me sooner if you were a major league baseball player!"

"Why? What would that have changed? It might have been better for you not to know. No pressure."

"But, but…"

"Listen, you said it yourself, kiddo. I was a big leaguer and had a good career, but those days are long gone. Now I'm just an old man who loves baseball as much as you do."

And then suddenly, there it was… the sadness in his eyes. It was a sadness I knew all too well.

Whether a person doesn't play baseball because they are not good enough or because they are too old, it produces the same melancholy I saw spread over his face and hide his smile.

It was that big smile that I had grown accustomed to. After that day, it still accompanied him every time we played baseball, but I will not forget the day the pain reached his eyes and stole that smile away. I will never forget that look, as if something of immense value was missing and irreplaceable. I never said it to him, but I understood the feeling.

We didn't just talk about baseball, George, and me. We talked about life. He once told me about his childhood. He said I reminded him a lot of his youth because he could see the same drive and passion he had. Like me, he had grown up in Willow Creek playing on a similar sandlot. And, just like me, every summer, Mr. Davis would gather with his friends to play and imagine what it would be like if they were playing in the major leagues.

He laughed a lot when he remembered one of his friends, Ben Driscoll. George told me how they had made the high school team together and then played against each other in college. As their careers became increasingly serious, they argued about which would first play in the Big Leagues. As he told me how much fun they had playing, talking baseball, and hanging out to watch the games, the shadow of sadness would disappear, replaced by the joy of recalling the glory years.

George felt he had less knowledge and experience and secretly worried that Ben was a much better player than he would ever be. But, in keeping with the lessons he passed on to the country sandlot, George believed that perseverance and dedication could bridge the gap between a man and talent or knowledge. Despite his worries, George made it to the big leagues after college while his friend, Ben, coached his high school team. Mr. Davis always insisted that, although they had the same dreams, Ben was quite different. Though George was thrilled to be signed into the major leagues, he couldn't hide his disappointment that Ben was not. Theirs was a true friendship.

Even the promise of money and fame did not shield George from sadness at not sharing the wealth with his dear friend.

Sitting and listening to these stories, I only wished to meet someone who meant what Ben meant to Mr. Davis. Someone who would still be happy for me even if his plans went awry. Of all the life-changing lessons I learned from George, that's what stuck with me the most. Instead of being jealous of his friend's success, Ben found a way to keep doing what made him happy while cheering his friend on to greater and greater success.

Sadly, as is always the way of nature, the summer days grew shorter, and the first hints of fall crept into the air with cooler breezes and leaves showing off their party colors. I knew my time with Mr. Davis was coming to an end. The sandlot games would soon give way to school, homework, holiday festivities, indoor activities, and other responsibilities. The magical world on the sandlot George and I had created together would fade into memory. I knew what Gene Kelly's character in the movie, *Brigadoon*, must have felt as the mystical city that materialized for one day every hundred years would vanish into the mists of time. Much like that extraordinary phenomenon, my connection with George

Davis was a rare, one-in-a-lifetime encounter. Our moments together embraced a magical quality, transient and cherished, evoking a profound sense of wonder and melancholy as the inevitable passage of time swept us apart.

As the days passed, Mr. Davis and I started saying our goodbyes. It was much too painful to tell them all at once. So, we chipped away at the tie that bound us together daily for the entire summer. We both knew it wasn't final, but it was clear that it wouldn't be the same. In the last days of hot weather and carefree living, we played less and talked more. I would ask Mr. Davis questions about his career, and he would answer everyone with that smile that never reached his eyes.

"What is it like being out there on the field with other players that are just as good as you? Were you ever scared?" I asked breathlessly.

"Scared? No, that's not the right word. Alert. I was alert. I remember one time…" his voice trailed off as a chuckle gathered stream in his chest.

The sound of his voice echoes in my ear, lingering, repeating the greatness of his words and the profoundness of his memories. The tales he wove remain, forever etched in my mind, as vivid as if they had unfolded before me merely yesterday. He narrated each story as though he were living them again in the present moment, imparting them to me with a strange intimacy, as if they were prized secrets meant solely for my ears. In that tender exchange, it felt as if I had the privilege of bearing witness to his stories as if no other soul had the right to hear them.

I leaned forward, weak with anticipation to hear what happened next.

"The crowd was silent. I could hear my opponent's breathing. The cool spring air was so tense you could cut it with a knife. Our pitcher had walked their lead-off hitter and then retired the next two hitters via strikeouts. Up to the plate stepped the always dangerous Frankie Corsetti. I was in awe of Mr. Corsetti as he was a favorite of my dad. He was also from Northern California, so it seemed fitting that my first major league game would be against one of Northern California's all-time greats. As Frankie stepped into the batter's box, I began to play a bit more up the middle to get the force out at second base, which would seal the win for us on opening day. Our pitcher went into his delivery and delivered a pitch when suddenly, the hitter hit a towering fly ball down the left field line. The runner on first took off on contact and was flying around the bases, sure to score the tying run if this ball landed in fair territory. The left fielder, third baseman, and I sprinted after the fly ball that seemed to be headed for no man's land. As if the baseball had eyes, it was just about to land in fair territory, and at that moment, I knew I would have to dive to catch the potential last out of the ball game.

In my head, I was analyzing all the possibilities and possible outcomes of that hit. It was as if time had stood still, I knew I had to catch that ball. Something told me to scream, "I've got it, I got it." With that, I lunged all out, fully extended with my glove stretched out... and as if it was written from above, the baseball fell directly into my glove for the game's final out!

As I bounced on the ground, the entire stadium went silent; I then looked into my glove as I prayed that my eyes would see the ball; I somehow heard my father say, "Prayers are for the church, son; the rest of the time is up to us." I pulled the ball out of my glove, and my teammates and the entire stadium erupted!"

I absorbed his words with the reverence reserved for a legend… a hero. Each tale he spun expanded the boundaries of my aspirations and instilled an unwavering belief in my potential. Just being in his presence as I recounted the days, the plays, the games, the looks, the sounds… he was a living testament and served as tangible evidence that one day I, too, could grace those magnificent stadiums. And, if fortune favored me, he would be there, cheering me on from the stands, urging me to push the boundaries even farther. *Someday*, I said to myself repeatedly as I envisioned that I might one day have the opportunity to make him proud, to showcase the person I had become under his influence, and to repay him for his guidance that had shaped me into a person capable of extraordinary accomplishments. "And what happened after, sir?" I said that day as I sat in rapt attention. I can still connect with the sensation of the illusion growing inside me, the warm feeling of becoming a part of his stories as if they were my own.

"We won, kiddo, we won. That's all."

He always ended his stories like that, as if it was so simple. They won, end of the story. I was so curious; why would he think it was so easy? Why did he talk of it as if it wasn't his hard work, nimble movements, and top-notch brain that had won him the day? I remember feeling bold that day, so I made the question go around in my head.

"But I don't understand, sir. That's all? You won! You should be telling me how that great play launched your career! It was surely not just 'only that.'"

"But it is, Jack. It was just that. We won, my career was established, and I was officially a big leaguer. I thought it would be the greatest day of my life. It wasn't, but it was good enough."

I remember my disbelief; I had never seen him so sad. The pain he was touching that day was like accidentally grabbing a hot iron. It was too sharp, too acute to hold. Those were the times when sorrow crept up his neck and rolled over his face, washing his smile away. The glory days were gone. The cheering crowds were gone. The athletic body was gone. Sorrow was all that remained. Dutifully, however, and faithfully, the smile always returned. For as long as I knew him, it came back, tiny, and shy, full of love and understanding. "You don't know it right now, kid, and it's good that you don't. But there are things more important than baseball."

And with that, he ruffled my head as my father would do and said:

"See you tomorrow, Jack."

A few years later, I would understand the reason for his sadness. Yes, he had been a great baseball player; he had a fantastic career and an extraordinary life. He married the love of his life and had a beautiful son. He spent weekends teaching his son to play baseball, practicing with him as he did with me. But he was hiding a secret from me that he had buried deep beneath his laughter.

He wasn't sure how to share his pain with me. So, he inched up to the subject slowly, like a runner taking his lead from first base.

"Seeing your son growing up and looking up to you is better than hitting a grand slam or throwing a no-hitter, young man," he said.

"Yes, sir?" I answered, unsure where the conversation was going. I was twelve. I had not even taken the time to think about having a son of my own.

"I love baseball more than anything because it bonded me and my son."

"That must have been so much fun for you. Does your son still play?"

Mr. Davis paused, hung his head, and took a deep breath before answering. "Life has its own plan and strange ways. They are not always the fairest. There is a lot of military tradition in my family, and my son wanted to be part of it. He joined the Navy and went to Vietnam. I was so proud of him. He wanted to serve his country. He was only a few years older than you when he enlisted. Sadly, he was killed in the line of duty. He never made it home."

I tried to imagine the pain he felt. But it was too troubling to conceive for more than a moment. How he had managed to live with it all these years remained a mystery to me.

"What- What did you do? I mean... after he died. How did you...?" I struggled to even form the words to ask the question.

"I felt as if I had lost everything. My joy of living was gone. I even stopped playing baseball. It was as if the game had never existed. It was too much to be near because so much was connected to my son. The war took all that from me. All the dreams, the plans, everything... ripped in pieces. When I saw kids playing, everyone reminded me of my son — what we had already lived together and the future we would never get to share."

I wanted to change the subject and give him a way to escape the pain of talking about it. But, at that moment, I couldn't stop myself from wondering why he was there with me — helping and teaching me.

"If it hurt so badly, Mr. Davis, why did you offer to train me?"

"Because, young man, I saw you out there on the field giving it your all day after day. I just passed by at first, thinking how determined you were. But then I noticed that you were always alone. No father out there showing you what to do or cheering you on. I don't know anything about your family. But you seemed to need a father, and I needed to remember how it felt to have a son."

We stood up on the sandlot side by side, both silent and pensive. We didn't speak another word, partly because of the sanctity of the moment and partly because there were no more words to say.

At that moment, I knew what I still know today; the lessons I learned with him would be carried with me forever. He shaped not only how I played baseball, but also how I saw life. Though I felt I had given my all to be a good student, I dug deeper, tried a little harder, and found a little more I could give. This man had set aside years of mourning to return to baseball through his time with me. I would surrender every ounce of strength to make his sacrifice worth it.

The friendship we forged that summer and the dreams we shared would remain part of me until my last day, fueling my determination to become the best player I could be, the best man I could be. And with a grateful heart and a newfound sense of purpose, I stepped up to the plate, eyes focused on the horizon, prepared to take the swing that would send his dreams soaring into the future.

CHAPTER 3

The Big Game

The summer drew to a close, and the first leaves began to fall over Willow Creek, California. The vibrant hues of green gave way to the warm tones of red, orange, and gold, painting a picturesque scene of transition and renewal. The air grew crisper, and the days grew shorter as the town embraced the arrival of autumn with open arms. The scent of pumpkin spice filled the cozy cafes, and the streets came alive with laughter and excited chatter as kids scurried up and down the streets, enjoying the final days of freedom before their lives would be consumed with school.

Families gathered at the local orchard, waiting for the ripening of rows and rows of apple trees. Soon it would be time to bake delicious pies and indulge in sweet treats. The community was excited, knowing the changing seasons brought a fresh wave of festivities and cherished traditions. Posters announcing fall festivals adorned the town square, with vibrant decorations lighting every corner and the promise of joyful melodies of live music filling the air. Farmers' markets displayed the season's bountiful harvest, offering a cornucopia of produce and crafts.

Neighbors exchanged warm greetings from the cool of their porches and yards, their breath visible in the crisp morning air. Against the backdrop of the rolling hills and the breathtaking colors of nature, Willow Creek, California, became a haven of warmth and unity. Though we lamented the coming end of summer, we reveled in the beauty the changing autumn brought. In Willow Creek, the transition from summer to fall was not just a shift in weather; it was a testament to the synchronized movement of community, connection, and the enduring spirit of a town that found joy in the simple wonders of life.

The chief subject for all my baseball crazed friends was the frenzied chatter of the yearly event that brought the whole town of Willow Creek together: the Annual End-of-Summer Sandlot Baseball Tournament. Kids from all corners of the city would gather to form teams and compete for the title of Sandlot Champions.

I was overcome with anticipation, realizing it was my moment to show everything I learned from Mr. Davis that summer and prove to my friends that I deserved a real place on the team. The excitement... the nerves... the chills running up and down my skin all signaled that it was time to make my case. Even though I was unsure if the improvements the other kids saw in me were enough for them to accept me on their team, I knew that I felt different with the ball, the bat, and the glove. Something had changed. How significant a change it was remained to be seen. No matter what, I would approach Tommy and ask for a prominent position. Besides, Mr. Davis insisted that I should.

"So, the big Annual game is coming up, I see. Posters everywhere."
"Yes, sir. A week from Saturday."
"Who's the captain of the team?"
"Well, Tommy, sort of."
"You tell him you're ready and want to play?"

"No, sir. I haven't."

"But you're going to?"

"Well, I… I guess so."

"You guess so?" Mr. Davis burst into a fit of laughter, holding his sides and slapping his knee while I stood there feeling entirely left out of the joke.

Mr. Davis eventually composed himself, wiping away tears of laughter. He looked at me with a mischievous glimmer in his eyes and said, "Son, let me tell you a little secret. When I was a kid, the traveling sideshow would come to town. The carney hawkers could sell ice to an Eskimo. They sold lotions and potions. All kinds of crazy foods.

They even sold what they claimed were shrunken heads. Do you know how they did it? Confidence! Confidence is the key to success in any endeavor. You can't 'guess' your way to victory. You've got to stride up to Tommy and say, 'I'm ready, and I'm going to give it my all.' You got me?"

His words resonated with me, and I nodded, determined to muster up the courage to approach Tommy.

Mr. Davis continued his tone now serious, "Remember, the game isn't just about winning or losing. It's about showing up, giving your best, and being part of a team. Win or lose, you'll have grown in ways you can't even imagine. If you don't believe in yourself, I'll loan you my belief in you. I've got plenty. So, no more guessing. You're a talented player. So, get going. Find Tommy. You walk right up to him and tell him you're ready."

"What? When? Now??" I panicked.

"Yep. Right now. No time like the present."

"But you and I haven't started practicing yet today."

"Well, what are you practicing for if you're not going to step up when an opportunity is staring you right in the face? Now get going. The train's leaving the station!" He burst into a loud snickering laugh.

The sound of his laughter nearly blew me off the sandlot as I took a deep breath and turned to leave.

Even after I crossed the road, I could still hear Mr. Davis's laughter echoing in the background; but this time, it no longer annoyed me. It energized me, reminding me to embrace life's challenges with a lighthearted spirit and unwavering self-belief.

Surprisingly, the more I walked — and the more he laughed — the greater the feeling of a surge of motivation coursed through my veins. I could still feel the pressure of his strong hand on my back minutes later as I approached Tommy's street. My steps quickened as my resolve grew. Then, in what felt like seconds, I was standing in front of Tommy's house.

Knock, knock, knock.

My hand trembled against the wooden screen door as I rapped my fist against it. But I stood still and strong, resisting the urge in my legs to run. This was my moment, and I was ready to face Tommy and make a case for my place on the team.

I replayed the many talks I had with Mr. Davis about how I should never set my mind to hearing a no for an answer. Nobody would ever give me a chance to show who I really was if I did.

"Jack! What's happening!" Tommy said with a smile as he opened the door and joined me on the porch. "How did you get here so fast? I just called your house less than a minute ago."

"I... uh..." Trembling and scared, I struggled to get the words out. "I..."

"Aw man, it sounds like something's wrong. What's up?"

"No!" I answered hastily. "Nothing's wrong. In fact, something is... I mean... it's good... It's..."

Tommy tilted his head to try to figure out what I was trying to say.

"Well, I mean...." I cleared my throat and imagined myself standing on Mr. Davis's shoulders, reaching ten feet tall. No matter what I thought, Mr. Davis believed in me. I would take him up on his offer to borrow his belief.

"Since you're the team captain," I said confidently, "I would like to be a player on the End of Summer team. I've been practicing every day and night. And I'm willing to practice all day long to get a spot. And I know—"

"Whoa! Whoa!" Tommy laughed. "Didn't you hear what I said?"

"Huh," I answered, realizing I had been rambling, unable to hear Tommy trying to interrupt.

"I said yes. You're good, man. Real good. You're the best outfielder in Walnut Creek in my opinion. That's why I was calling you. You're in!"

I can't explain how I felt when he said that one magic word: Yes. I couldn't believe it. I still don't. An exhilaration rose from the bottom of my heart and sent shockwaves through my body. I was the kid who was always on the sidelines, the one no one wanted to play with, the one that stayed until the sun was gone entirely, the one who had been gifted with an angel from above to push me. I made it. I thanked Tommy and ran home, but I am sure my feet never touched the ground.

* * * * *

The Willow Creek Sluggers. That was the name given to the team formed to play in the end-of-summer game. The most talented players in Willow Creek were recruited to play. And there I was… a veritable rookie in the middle of it all. I went to the first practice hoping and praying that I would not hurt the team with my immaturity and lack of experience. But, after the first practice, the team members were thrilled to have me.

Well, almost all of them that is. There was a guy named Jimmy Pearson who lived at the opposite end of town on the team. I didn't know him personally, only by reputation, and what a reputation it was. He was 12, but looked like he was 18. He was already 6 feet tall and looked like he could grow a beard in three days if he wanted to. He was a pitcher and a first baseman and legends had spread for a couple of summers that he once hit a 435-foot home run that smashed a car window across the railroad tracks. If anyone was going to make the majors from our little town, Jimmy was that guy. He had a temper to match his power hitting, though. If baseball didn't work out, he could probably be equally successful at boxing or pro wrestling.

Jimmy's best buddy was a guy named Kyle Richardson. Kyle had been the Sluggers' starting centerfielder the summer before, but he had broken his wrist when he got hit by a fastball and missed six weeks of spring and summer ball. When he finally got back on the field, he couldn't find his stroke again and he had been left off the roster. Jimmy had gone out of his way to tell me several times that the only reason I was on the team was because Kyle had a broken wrist, and a couple of times he said he hoped "nothing bad happened to me."

After Tommy overheard his angry words one day, he pulled me aside and told me not to believe it.

"Even if Kyle hadn't broken his wrist, you'd still be starting, Jack," he said. "Kyle would have been sitting on the bench after the way you came on this year.

Jimmy had respect and most of the other guys feared him, but they didn't like him. Turns out Tommy was right. The rest of the team was definitely liking the way I played.

They even said their lineup was more athletic than ever with me and my new skills! It was unbelievable for the 12-year-old me to hear such high praise. I admit my chest was full of pride, and my confidence soared, causing me to play even better. We continued to train until the big day came.

We were all amateurs in the grand scheme of things. We needed a coach. Our so-called training was getting together the day after to play and play and play again. We knew, if nothing else, that we had to learn how to play together. But, having spent those summer days with Mr. Davis, I found myself giving tips to my teammates. Everything my mentor had taught me was fresh in my mind, and I could see the field in a way none of the other kids did. As I explained suggestions or showed them certain drills, they looked at me amazed. I was no longer the Jack Thompson they had known since childhood. Suddenly I was elevated to a respected and knowledgeable player the team looked to for guidance and trusted as a member of the group. The only guy I didn't approach was Jimmy. I wanted to. I didn't want to have this bad blood between us because we'd need everyone playing at their best if we were going to accomplish something special. I had seen a hitch in his swing from my lessons with Mr. Davis. I knew that if Jimmy addressed the hitch, he'd be really hard to get out, but any time I came near him, he fixed a stare on me that looked like pure hate, so I kept my distance.

The calendar inched closer and closer to the day of the big game, and the team felt confident that we had congealed as a unit. A few days before the tournament started, we talked about positions, player changes, who should start the game on the field, who would pitch, who would bat last, and so on.

Then, the unthinkable happened.

"I think Jack should be the captain," Tommy said.

The words rang out so loud in my ears; everything else being said sounded muffled, like everyone was suddenly underwater. I remember it today as if it just happened moments ago. I can still recall the sensation of my blood running cold like that day. The moment was surreal, and I struggled to identify where I had gone from being the worst player to being nominated by the "de facto captain" to replace him as the team leader. For the first few seconds, I lost the ability to speak. In the corner of my mind, I heard Jimmy swearing at the suggestion. I wanted to refuse, to say that what Tommy was saying was crazy and that he should be the chosen captain. I wanted to protest that he couldn't fill that position, that his shoes were too big to fill, and that Tommy was the better choice. More than anything, I wanted to refuse before anyone tried to talk some sense into Tommy and say out loud that I wasn't good enough. But while I was still caught up in amazement, it happened.

"Yes! Jack should do it!" one shouted.

"I agree," another said.

"It makes sense. Jack has been helping all of us these days to improve our game!" said another kid.

Sadly, all these years later, I don't remember the names of these kids who were singing my praises and filling me with so much positive energy with their kind words. I wish I could remember them all because their words changed my life.

As they continued to talk about the idea of my leading them, I considered the possibility that I had fallen into a dreamlike state. It had all been a dream. Perhaps even Mr. Davis wasn't real. How could it be that a kid with no talent and a lot of heart should catch his eye and earn his mentorship? Then, after weeks and weeks of practice standing in a circle with boys, I admired hearing them choose me as their leader. Today it still feels like a dream to me. They trusted me. They believed in my ability.

It was the one thing I always wanted.

I went home that afternoon feeling intoxicated as if I was walking, sleepy, still trying to figure out if it was a bad joke, and unable to speak. I found my parents in the kitchen when I walked through the door.

"Hey, son," my father said, walking toward me to tousle my hair. But when he saw the look on my face, he stopped short.

"Jack?" Mom asked with a worried look on her face, "is everything OK? You're as pale as a sheet!"

"Yeah, boy. You look like you've seen a ghost."

God knows I did; it was the spirit of my dreams and hopes coming alive! It was the death of my doubts and the rising of my aspiration.

"They picked me. Me!"

"Who are you talking about?"
"The team! I'm the captain of the End of Summer team!"

I'm not sure either one of them really knew what that meant. They had tried to keep up with my baseball career as best they could, especially when they began realizing that I had gotten good at it, but terms like "team captain" didn't really register with them. However, my tone of voice and the thrill in my voice were enough to sell them. I had accomplished something amazing, and they were going to show me that they were truly proud of me.

We celebrated that day in a way we never had before. My father was uncharacteristically giddy. My mother stopped everything she was doing to throw her arms around me and dance me around the room. We hugged, high-fived, back-slapped, and repeated how amazing it was.

However, with the celebration over and the shock subsiding, the moment's reality hit me. I was thrilled to just be a player on the team. I didn't care if we won or lost. I was truly honored just to be invited to play. But, as the captain, we had to win!

* * * * *

The weekend of the baseball tournament finally arrived, and the atmosphere was charged with anticipation and excitement. The first thing that caught my eye was the sea of vibrant colors. As I stepped out onto the field, I saw it was meticulously prepared for the event, stretched out in a luscious green expanse of freshly cut grass surrounding the sandlot. The chalk lines were sharp and distinct, marking the bases and outfield boundaries. The pearly white bases gleamed in the sunlight, the old homemade bases replaced by ones fresh from the plastic, their white surfaces contrasting against the rich earth tones of the infield.

The bleachers on the sidelines were crammed with the Willow Creek community, other families and friends, and fans of the opposing teams. They wore colorful jerseys, hats, and T-shirts, each proudly representing their team. The air was abuzz with the cheerful banter and laughter of the crowd. Younger brothers and sisters ran around,

The Big Game·

their youthful energy adding to the lively atmosphere. Banners and flags fluttered in the breeze, displaying team logos and colorful designs, heightening the festive feel.

The crack of the bat echoed through the field as a batter connected with a practice pitch, followed by the cheers and applause of the spectators who had come early. Coaches shouted instructions and encouragement from the dugouts, their voices carrying into the stands and across the field. Tommy's dad was our coach, but really just in name only. We knew each other so well and practiced together so often that the only thing a grown-up coach could do was take the lineup card to home plate and ask the umpire for an explanation if a bad call went against us. Tommy's dad kept his pep talk to a minimum, but he did have one motivational speech that always got us going - a win meant pizza and ice cream after the game!

The thump of a well-caught ball hitting the leather of a mitt resonated in my ear. I was overcome, for the first time, knowing this was precisely where I belonged.

I tried to stay calm, knowing that the games would soon begin. I regretted not grabbing a bite to eat earlier as the unmistakable smells of delicious ballpark food filled the air and rumbled my stomach. The aroma and sizzle of hot dogs on the grill mingled with the buttery scent of freshly popped popcorn. The enticing fragrance of cotton candy and caramel apples wafted from the concession stands, tempting my senses. But I could eat later.

I was there to prove something to myself, and my team.

I had been in this same patch of clay and grass every day for weeks. But this once humble sandlot had undergone a remarkable transformation. It now stood as a vibrant hub of excitement. The passion and energy radiating from the players, families, and spectators brought life to the once-quiet space. The combination of sights, sounds, and smells created an immersive experience, making the baseball tournament an unforgettable event for everyone involved.

All the parents were there, except for mine. I was used to their absence, but it was disappointing anyway. They understood how important this was to me when I was elected captain. But, just as quickly, the celebration faded, and they returned to their busy lives, leaving me to face this moment alone. I understood that they had to work. The bills didn't stop mounting because I was having a big day. But… this was my big day. My twelve-year-old brain couldn't fathom why, just this once, they couldn't put me first.

Years later, when I was an adult, I realized they didn't want to be absent. We needed the money to help me make my future dreams come true. When you were immigrants like my mom and dad were, and you hadn't gotten an American education, you tended to do the jobs that most other people didn't want to. That meant you didn't get days off for vacation or when you were sick like most parents. It's probably why my folks were so grateful when holidays like Christmas and New Year's and the 4th of July rolled around. Nobody worked then. But kids can be selfish sometimes. Selfish and jealous that it seemed everyone else had family but me. I didn't want to understand that I was the only one without a family to cheer me on.

In a flash, however, my disappointment quickly changed to joy when, in the distance, seated in an old, battered chair, I saw Mr. Davis. He was trying to act nonchalantly as if he had no intention of watching the game. But he couldn't fool me. After all this time, I knew him well. I knew he was there to see me, to silently cheer me on. The mere sight of him was all I needed to regain my joy. And that joy gave me strength.

The Big Game

Then, the Sluggers' first game started. It was a breeze; our team executed plays with precision and skill, easily beating our opponents by a final score of 12-1. We were never behind, and I had felt like a captain - going 4 for 6 at the plate with 3 runs driven in and a pair of steals. I didn't just take all the pats on the back though, I was captain and the biggest voice in the dugout, rooting loudly for my teammates and picking them up on the rare occasion when something didn't work out for us. I remember feeling Mr. Davis looking at me; even though my back was turned to him, I could feel the warmth of that proud smile and the sad eyes above it. I functioned well in my role as captain, cheering my teammates and sharing my passion and dedication.

As the day wore on, the competition grew fiercer. The Sluggers faced off against more skilled and experienced teams, but our determination never wavered. My newfound confidence and abilities shone through as I made diving catches and hit balls that soared as if bound for the sun. I was no longer the awkward, uncoordinated kid I had been at the beginning of the summer; I was a leader and a force to be reckoned with on the field.

The Sluggers earned our place in the final championship game, facing off against our biggest rivals: the formidable Oakwood Tigers. The Tigers were known for their aggressive play and had won the tournament for the past three years. They were confident and unshakable players. Worse, they were smug, convinced they would claim the title again.

As the game began, the tension was palpable. Both teams played with determination and grit, each run scored and caught carrying the weight of our dreams. The lead shifted back and forth, with neither team able to establish a clear advantage. When we got to the bottom of the ninth, the Tigers had used an error to take a 5-4 lead. It was our last chance to either tie the game and send it to extra innings or when it outright. You could tell players from both teams were really worn out. I didn't know how much longer we could keep giving 100% without the pressure cracking us.

We were down to our last out and Jimmy Pearson was up next, with me waiting on deck. Jimmy had a home run earlier in the day, and I was 3-for-3. The other team knew that they couldn't give him a pitch to hit, or he'd blast another home run and tie the game. They had all of their outfielders playing deep and their infielders were too. Jimmy was a big kid and didn't run very fast, so they clearly wanted to get him to ground out. He wasn't very patient, so even if they threw him a lot of balls out of the strike zone, he'd keep swinging, trying to be a hero.

At that moment, I remembered something Mr. Davis had told me once, an old story from his playing days, and I got a big smile that I quickly hid. Just before Jimmy stepped up to the plate, I asked Tommy's dad to call timeout. Jimmy looked annoyed and came back to where me, Tommy, and his dad were all standing in a huddle.

"What's the big idea?" he complained. "You ruined my routine!"
"You should bunt," Tommy replied.

Jimmy choked with laughter. "BUNT?! Are you crazy? I can tie the game with one swing, buntings for girls!" Tommy's dad didn't know as much about baseball as us, but he was still a grownup and his voice mattered.

"Think about it, son. They won't give you a pitch to drive because they know how powerful you are. All their infielders are way back. Drop a bunt and you can walk to first. The whole crowd will laugh at those dopes for falling for it."

Jimmy loved home runs, but he also enjoyed embarrassing other players. He nodded and said, "Good idea, I'll humiliate them!"

He turned and walked back to the plate.

"Nice idea, Jack," Tommy said under his breath. "Wish you could have taken credit for it, though."

"He'd never take my advice," I said softly. "But if he gets on, I'll make them pay."

Just like Mr. Davis told me in his stories, the air was heavy. Hundreds and hundreds of people surrounding the sandlot fell silent as Jimmy strode to the plate. He took his stance, waggled his bat, and as the pitch came to him - an off-speed pitch low and inside, he dropped his bat at the last moment and bunted it down the third-base line.

The crowd gasped as one, and Jimmy lumbered down the line. It was one of the funniest sights I'd ever seen on the baseball diamond. The third baseman stood there with his mouth wide open. The pitcher was doing the same thing. Eventually they both ran at the ball as it trickled down along the third-base path. They both reached for it at the same time and collided with each other in a jumble of arms and legs. Jimmy heard the commotion and didn't even hesitate, turning the corner and chugging to second base without a throw. The crowd roared in delight and laughed in appreciation. Our biggest slugger had just hit a 23-foot double.

Suddenly, just like in so many of the stories I had played out in my mind, it all came down to my last at bat. My performance in this critical moment would decide whether we won or lost. The expectations of my team and community were like elephants resting on my chest. But I remembered Mr. Davis's words: "Baseball is as much a game of the mind as it is of the body, kiddo."

I took a deep breath and let the wave of calm determination wash over me. Then I got in the batter's box and got in my stance and looked out at the pitcher. I tapped my bat on the ground to steel my nerves and then suspended it over my shoulder, waiting for the perfect moment to strike. The first pitch hissed as it slammed into the catcher's mitt, " steerike... " the umpire exclaimed. I made sure I was ready for the next pitch, swung so hard my helmet fell off, and now there were no balls and two strikes. I looked around the field and saw the opposing team preparing to celebrate.

I had to be smart now. No good pitcher ever throws another strike when he's ahead 0-2. All my mental work with Mr. Davis was rising to the top of my brain right now. The next pitch was way outside, and I watched it go without even moving. The one after that looked good when it left his hand, then the bottom dropped out. The next one was way outside, and now the pressure was all on the pitcher. He had gone from 0-2 to a full count, and if he walked me, he was walking the potential winning run.

I took a deep breath, and the pitcher went into his windup, and when that pitch came, I swung with all my might, connecting with the ball, and sending it soaring high into the sky. As I raced around the bases, I could hear the cheers of my friends, families, and teammates urging me on.

As if written by a Hollywood scriptwriter, young Jack crossed home plate to the roar of an adoring crowd. I had done more than just win the game. I had proven to myself and everyone else that I had what it took to be a solid contributing player. And, I had honored the sacrifice of a great man who gave up his summer to teach me. With the love and support of my mentor, friends, and community, young Jack Thompson had risen from the humblest of beginnings to become, for the time being, a true sandlot hero.

And that is a feeling I will always keep in a special place in my heart and memories.

A New Challenge

As the leaves turned golden and the air grew crisp, life in Willow Creek began to return to its normal rhythm. The excitement of the summer baseball tournament started to fade. It was replaced by the bustle of school, homework, and fall activities. But for me, the memories of that magical summer and the championship game triumph have always remained deep inside me.

Like any 12-year-old, I didn't like going to school. Yes, going meant spending the morning with my friends. Besides, as my mother used to say, it was where I would learn to be the person I wanted to become. But all I wanted was to keep playing baseball, not sit in a chair for hours listening to boring teachers tell me things that never interested me.

Later in life, I heard myself saying those things my mother used to say to my sons, and I won't forget their faces of disagreement that matched my own when I was their age. They didn't know I understood the feeling, that I was young once, and swore I wouldn't repeat what my parents said to me when I had kids.

Back then, baseball consumed every corner of my mind. It was all I wanted to do, and I couldn't wait until the summer to start again. That prayer was answered when, one day, while walking home from school, something caught my attention — a flyer on a community bulletin board announcing the tryouts for the Willow Creek Junior League Baseball team. The Junior League was a competitive league for the most talented young players in the area. Being selected was a prestigious honor and one I could only dream of.

My heart began running fast as I considered the possibility. The sandlot games were fun and a chance to test my skills against the best of the best. This was much bigger. However, Mr. Davis helped me learn that if I only allowed myself to dream small, everything I would achieve would be small by default. If I wanted to go further, I had to dream bigger. Even if I didn't accomplish my goals, at least I would have put everything into it.

Yet, a part of me doubted I was ready for what came next. With Mr. Davis's guidance and hard work, I became a formidable player, but could I compete at the Junior League level? I wasn't sure about the answer, but I had to try.

I walked home thinking about how I would ask my parents. I knew they supported my dream, but I was curious if they would approve of me being on a team during the school season. I had to prove to them I was responsible enough to continue my studies and baseball — that my will was strong enough.

They weren't home yet, and I felt too nervous to just sit around waiting for them, so I decided to keep walking. I felt so nervous I couldn't think clearly. I knew I wanted baseball, but I was curious to know if my parents could find a way to afford it. I had practiced my speech to them as I walked but it never seemed good enough. Unfortunately, I was so busy working out each sentence in my head that I wound up losing track of time. By the time I actually made it back home, the sun was dipping low in the sky. They were already home when I arrived. There I was again, standing in the middle of the room, crackling with nerves.

"Where were you, Jack?" my mother said. "We were worried; you never arrive this late!"

"I know, Mom. I'm sorry, I lost track of time, and—"

"We were so worried," Dad chimed in. "I even went to look for you! But you were nowhere to be found!"

"I know, Dad, I know. But if you let me explain…"

"Oh no, young man," Dad scolded. "You are grounded. You'll think twice about giving us a scare like this next time."

"No, Dad. No, please. I have something important to tell you. I was out walking because I didn't know how to say it to you. I walked around trying to figure it out!" I didn't mean to raise my voice. But I couldn't believe this was happening to me. I thought it must have been a joke, a terrible one. I begged, "Please. Please. Listen to me."

"No, Jack. I won't listen to you right now because I need you to understand that you cannot do this again."

"I understand, Dad, please…"

"Jack, listen to your father," said my mom.

I looked at her with pleading eyes, hoping she would see I needed an ally.

"I know this is a small town," Dad interjected, "and Willow Creek is safe for the kids to play without worrying. Going missing for such a long time may not be a big deal for you, but it is for us."

At some point, I stopped listening to him. After all, nothing ever happened in Willow Creek, absolutely nothing. I looked at my father as if he had lost his mind. What could happen to me? I had spent early morning and late-night hours on the sandlot and came home safely. They had no reason to react like that. And I was sure that punishing me wasn't fair!

As a father, I understand now how afraid they must have been. I know it's different from where you live or how safe and calm the area is. There is something profound and rooted in parenting that makes them go nuts the moment they don't know where their kids are. It doesn't have to be rational; it just reflects their love and urge to protect.

I know my parents loved me no matter what. Still, when I was younger, I thought some decisions they made were just to make me angry, to show me who was in charge at home — like what happened that day.

Parents have different ways to show their love for their children. Some give kisses and hugs, others encourage them, others let them be themselves, and some don't know how to show it. Yet, they all have one thing in common: They do whatever it takes to make their children happy and keep them safe. No one ever gives them an instruction manual on how to show their love.

I remember going to bed raging that night. I was furious. Now I laugh at how exaggerated my emotional reaction was at that time. I thought I wouldn't talk to them if they didn't listen to me anymore. They would regret punishing me without giving me a chance to explain myself. I had reasons for being late, and they didn't seem to care.

As children, we tend to think of ourselves as adults. We assume the difference is that we are shorter, younger, and have less money! We believe that we can make our own decisions and are right regardless of what others think.

If you think about it, it's pretty funny how we get upset at the world when our parents try to protect us. We sense that trying to "hurt them back" by not talking to them, because we cannot see that scolding or punishing us is the only way they know to make us understand that we are wrong.

I was still angry the next day. I went to school with the most somber expression. When my friends asked if something had happened, I answered simply: "My parents don't understand me." That sparked a spirited teenage conversation in which we all agreed on one thing: Our parents didn't know how to understand us, they only thought about themselves, and everything was very unfair.

What can I say? Teenagers' daily life. Full of drama!

As silly as it sounds, I was much more relieved when I got home that afternoon after learning that all my friends had the same problem as me. The feeling of being understood by your peers can help the anger subside. I arrived on time; as expected, my parents weren't home yet. So, I spent the time until they came doing my homework and being a good boy so that, when they got over their anger, I would have a chance to talk to them and, hopefully, be allowed to take the trials. Even if *I wouldn't talk to them anymore*, I had to speak to them this once, just to prove I was responsible and centered enough for them to trust me.

Obviously, I didn't stop talking to my parents. Not then, never. When they arrived, I tried to seem as angry as possible, to show them my disagreement with their rules through my ice-cold indifference. As you can imagine, it didn't work.

We sat at the table, having dinner, when my mother asked me:

"So, Jack, what did you want to tell us yesterday that was so important?"

"Like if you cared," I said it so quietly that I thought no one could hear me, but clearly, my father did. The look he gave me screamed, "Respect your mother, or you'll be grounded until you're 80!" That look still makes me panic today.

"It wasn't anything, Mom."

"Really?" she said. "It really seemed truly important yesterday."

I had to choose whether to risk a straight no if they were still too angry with me or to stay quiet until the tension subsided. But the day of the tryouts was near, so it was a now-or-never situation.

"I mean... yesterday, on my way back home, I saw a flier for the Willow Creek Junior League Baseball team tryouts," I spoke so fast that I still didn't know how they could understand a thing. "And before you say anything, you must know... Well... I know, okay? I know. School is important. But baseball is my dream. I want to take a chance and try out for the team. I know it will be challenging, and I still have a lot to learn, but I want to give myself a chance to dream bigger. I won't disappoint you; I promise. I will do my homework every day, and I will keep my grades up. I will study even more on the weekends! But please, please. Let me try."

Then I breathed.

For a moment, it felt as if time had frozen. I looked from one parent to the other, studying their faces, trying to predict what they would say. That may be the day I met what real fear looked like. I was sure

A New Challenge

my heart would jump out of my chest if I had to wait another second for their response!

"That was all? All this drama... just for that?"

When my father said those words, I felt my world falling apart; I was sure I had miscalculated and thought I should have waited; it was too soon. I felt the pressure in my chest, trying to anticipate my parents' response.

"Of course, you can go to the tryouts, son," my dad said. "I'm sure that, after all, you have learned this summer with Mr. Davis, you will be selected for the team."

I couldn't believe it. That easy? No questions, no warnings, no threats that *you can forget about baseball forever if you don't keep on with your studies.* I had to be dreaming. That had to be a joke. I had been so nervous, and just for this.

"Don't look at us like that, son," my mother added. "What did you think we were going to say? You have always spent the whole summer talking about nothing but baseball. Do you really think we didn't realize how much you love the game?"

I couldn't believe my ears. I was not aware of how much I had talked about it with my parents, perhaps because, to some extent, my pre-adolescent mind didn't want to understand that when I spoke, they were really listening.

And there it was. My parents supported me, even if my chances of making the team were small. The fact that a team of that caliber might select me was minute, but I had their support. They even talked about how they could drive me to training and watch me play on weekends. I guess they felt guilty about missing me winning the big tournament.

It was all anyone in town talked about for a while, and the fact that neither one of them had been there for it had been noticed in the hours, days, and weeks after my clutch home run.

That night I felt unstoppable. With my parents behind me and Mr. Davis cheering me on from the sidelines while continuing to give me pointers from time to time, I would have the confidence to compete for an opportunity to play on an elite-level team.

* * * * *

The day of the tryouts arrived, and I was surrounded by talented players from all over the town. The competition was fierce, with each kid highlighting their skills in hopes of securing a spot on the team. But I put everything I had learned from Mr. Davis into practice, focusing on my footwork, swing, and mental game.

Time flew by that day. Once the tryouts ended, the coaches gathered the anxious players to announce the final roster. The tension in the air was thick as the names were read aloud, one by one. I could see the coach getting close to the end of the list of names on the sheet of paper he held in his hand.

Ethan Anderson...
Benjamin Reynolds...
James Alexander...
Noah Wright...
Jimmy Pearson ...
Jack... Jack Mitchell...

I held my breath. The coach read off the name Jack, but it wasn't me. All hope seemed lost. And he was lowering the paper before reading the last name.

And lastly, Jack Thompson.

I let out a breath and a silent cheer. I had made the team.

I will never forget my first practice before my first season as a Willow Creek Junior League team player. Nor will I forget the feeling of knowing that I truly belonged and that all of my hard work had paid off. It all reminded me of why I had fallen in love with the game in the first place.

Baseball is about hope and promise. It is not just about balls and bats, gloves, and bases. It is called the American pastime for a reason. It is part of the American dream that a kid from a small town in Northern California could prove his worth and become a valued member of the team. Baseball is the epitome of realized potential.

CHAPTER 5

A Chance Encounter

During that first season, I found myself tested in ways I would have never imagined. Everything was more intense and intricate on this new team, and the stakes were higher than ever. I held onto the lessons I learned from Mr. Davis, but I still needed help to adapt to the intense demands of the team's season.

I remember, at some point, missing the simpler days of playing in the sandlot back when it was all just for fun. I couldn't help but make comparisons; in the sandlot, you knew that even though the other team was your opponent, they were still your friends. There was a feeling of camaraderie that was missing on the Junior team. Despite being a team, we all needed to shine and be noticed to show that we were the best players. There was no room for jokes. Games were played at a different level and intensity — where winning was the only option.

Guys didn't root for you as much at this level. Sure, we all wanted to win, but over time I started getting the feeling that most guys would rather go 3-for-4 and hit a home run in a game we lost than go 0-for-2 in a game we won. The thing was, if you made it to this level, it meant that a lot of people were starting to think you had a future in baseball.

It meant you were definitely going to play in high school, and if you continued on this path, you had a good shot to play in college, too. And if you did well in college, well, you know what that might mean - the ultimate dream, playing baseball professionally.

But the higher up the ladder you went, the fewer spots there were on each team. Everyone could play at the neighborhood sandlot, even if you just sat around the dugout 99 days out of 100, you were still practicing, hanging out, and having fun.

Hanging out and laughing was only for before and after practice, now. You are working on your basic skills and learning advanced ones now. It wasn't good enough that you could hit the ball hard, you had to read the defense and know how to hit the ball against the shift. It wasn't good enough to be a pitcher with a really great fastball. There were guys on this level who could hit the ball as hard as you could throw it. It wasn't enough to be just "decent" in the field. You had to understand your defensive assignments, but those of everyone else as well so you could work together as a unit.

I remember thinking that I wasn't up to the task when, sometimes, my confidence wavered. Despite everything I had learned that summer with Mr. Davis, it still wasn't enough. The pitchers threw harder, the fielder's moves were more agile, and the pressure to perform felt more significant. And yet, his words were still fresh in my mind, along with that constant reminder that to get where I wanted to go, I had to have focus, discipline, and an attitude that showed that giving up wasn't an option.

I hadn't come so far to doubt myself again and was ready to face any challenge that came my way. The constant reproach of not *being enough* would stay with me throughout my career. I was always trying to prove that I was better than that.

A Chance Encounter

One afternoon, the training was grueling. My heartbeat in my ears, deafening me. My arms caught fire and burned from my shoulder to my wrists. No matter how hard I breathed, the air wasn't going down to my lungs. I knew that sacrifice was necessary if I wanted to play at the higher levels of the game, and I was willing to face it repeatedly. But that afternoon, I thought that with just one more minute on the field, my body would collapse.

At the end of the practice and after recovering a little from exhaustion, I decided to go to the sandlot to clear my mind. It's always good to put things in perspective by going to the place where it all began.

Even though the summer wasn't that long ago at that point, it felt like ages had passed for me. And yet, everything was the same as always. With the sun setting, casting a warm glow over the dusty field, I lost myself in thought.

I loved baseball more than anything in this world. I still do. But at the age of twelve, it was my whole life. Baseball was the first thing I thought of when I woke up, and it was my last thought before going to sleep; I couldn't help it. I loved it so much that sometimes, I could hardly breathe.

I had the illusion that if I could become the best baseball player, I could prove to my parents that I was worthy of their time and that every effort and every sacrifice they made was worth it. I realize that I needed to bring the same effort to my new team that I used to when I was trying to make the neighborhood squad. Skills weren't enough. I needed to outwork everyone.

One day, I went to practice and stayed long after the team had left practicing like I had done on the sandlot. I would have stayed there all night in the middle of the field if I hadn't heard footsteps approaching me. When I turned around, I was surprised to see Taylor, a former sandlot teammate who hadn't made the cut for the Junior League team. Even though we hadn't seen much of each other since the summer, we greeted each other warmly and started to catch up on the events of the past few months.

"I'm glad you made the team, Jack. After all you did this summer, you deserved it," said Taylor.

"Thanks, buddy." I smiled at him.

We sat on the edge of the field, discussing the pranks and jokes we had pulled on each other during the summer.

"I miss this so much, Taylor," I said, almost crying from laughing so hard. "The Junior League is everything I have imagined, but every training is so serious. There is no place for things like that."

"What do you mean, Jack?"

"I mean, it's not that I don't like to play baseball anymore. But some days like today, I don't remember *why* I liked it so much, you understand?"

Taylor looked at me and then to the field. He drew in his breath and smiled as he let it out. It was one of those friendly smiles that kept secrets you weren't even aware you had.

"I get it, Jack. I was so disappointed when I didn't make the cut for the team. So disappointed. Being in that team was all I wanted since I was five, and I started to play with my father on the weekends."

I felt a sharp pain in my back. It was a twinge of envy, seeing others have time with their dads I could only dream of. I loved my parents, of course, but when I heard other kids talking about theirs, I couldn't help but succumb to jealousy. I couldn't shake off that slight wave of disappointment that crawled up my back like a snake ready to bite me on the neck as a reminder that I couldn't have those treasured moments with them.

Taylor continued, "But after seeing you and the others play… maybe it is a good thing that I didn't make the team."

"Why do you say that, Taylor? You're such a good player. You should be the one on the team, not me. You were one of those who I looked up to, always smiling, always cheering the others. All I wanted to earn this summer was your respect — for you all to know I was no longer the worst player in the sandlot!"

"Thank you, man. I really appreciate your words. But you deserve to be on the team. I could never do what you did this summer."

I looked at him as if he had lost his mind. *What did I do that summer?* All I did was play with them.

Taylor saw the confusion on my face. "You really thought we never noticed how hard you practiced? Every day when we left the sandlot, you stayed in, Jack. We all knew. And we all admired how you stayed there and practiced, and practiced, and practiced some more. You spent the whole summer training as if the sandlot was the league! We were there just to have fun, but you… it was different for you. When I told my dad that you made the cut and not me, he was happy for you, but I was a bit angry. Until I understood."

"Understood? What did you understand?"

"That I have next year, Jack. And the next after that. And the one that comes after. I have all the time in the world to play. This doesn't mean I gave up; I just realized there's more to life than baseball. It's something you should remember."

I pulled back. I knew there was more than just baseball in life; it was only that I loved baseball so much that occasionally I just forgot.

"I think it's okay to do other things, too. For it not to be so serious all the time. Spending the summer playing ball was only really to have fun with you guys, you know?"

I thought about Taylor's words as I walked home that evening and many after that day. When I reached my house, I leaned in to say hello and let my family know I was back. Then I sat on the porch and looked at the sky painted with the setting sun's colors. I tried to comprehend Taylor's words that were jumping around in my head. I didn't realize at that moment the importance of what Taylor said, it was a life lesson. I discovered that in my quest to become the best player I could be, I had lost sight of the joy and camaraderie that had drawn me to baseball in the first place.

But I also knew it was too late to return to the sandlot's carefree days. What I could do was carry the spirit of those days with me as I faced the challenges of the Junior League. As Taylor said, I'd have all the time in the world to play, but something told me that *that* was my year. It had been part of the events that brought me to the league.

If I hadn't stayed late in the field each evening after everyone had left, I wouldn't have met Mr. Davis. If I hadn't met Mr. Davis, I wouldn't have begun to be friends with Taylor and the others. I wouldn't have played on the team during the tournament if I hadn't been friends with them. If I hadn't played in that tournament, I wouldn't have had enough confidence to try out for the Junior Team. I learned how far I had come because I made the cut.

I couldn't go back to that point — baseball was everything I wanted, and for the first time, the dream didn't seem to be slipping through my fingers.

With renewed determination, I trained to excel on the field. I rediscovered the passion that had fueled my love for the game. I began to find a balance between the intensity of the Junior League and the simple joy of playing with my friends on the sandlot.

I was really tight during our early-season games. Every time I threw the ball in, if it wasn't a perfect laser beam, it made me mad. I thought I was a good enough hitter that I should never be fooled by a pitch. If I hit a line drive that someone made a great play on, I was OK with it, but if it was a lazy pop fly or a routine grounder, I beat myself up about it. Even drawing a walk frustrated me. Coaches liked walks, because the more runners you have on base, the more likely good things were to happen. I found them frustrating because I was always chomping at the bit to smash the ball as hard as I could. If they walked me, I would immediately look for a shot to steal second base.

After my talk with Taylor, I was able to relax just a bit. The memories of the sandlot summer made me take a second look at baseball and remind myself that it still was just a game, despite being one I was passionate about with every bone in my body. I wasn't going to get a hit every time I was at the plate. Heck, even the season Ted Williams hit .406, he still made an out 59.4% of the time! I wasn't going to get to every ball hit to the outfield. I was the fastest kid on the team, maybe the fastest in the city, but there were still limits to how far I could run before a ball hit the ground. I made a point to cheer for my teammates when they did well, even if they didn't return the sentiment. If a guy made a great play and robbed me of a hit, occasionally I'd tip my cap to him. All these guys loved baseball just as much as I did. What kind of guy would I be if I didn't acknowledge their greatness as well?

As the season drew to a close, I felt a sense of pride in how far I had come, both as a player and a person. I faced adversity, learned valuable lessons from my mentor and friends, and grew physically and mentally stronger. And as I stepped up to the plate for the final game of the season, I knew that I was ready to face whatever challenges lay ahead, both on and off the field, because from the bottom of my heart, I knew there was no other place on Earth I wanted to be.

CHAPTER 6

A Mentor's Wisdom

The first season ended, and I continued reflecting on everything I learned from Mr. Davis.

Even if my game hadn't improved the way it did, his lessons would still have changed how I saw movement on the field and would have been instrumental in shaping my view of the world. I was no longer that boy who only sought the approval of his teammates; I had begun to transform into the man I would be one day.

Mr. Davis taught me to stop, be patient, and observe the movement of others to inspire my own. He also taught me to make my own decisions on and off the field, to speak up for myself, and to think. Mr. Davis led me to understand the importance of footwork in baseball, to improve my grip on the bat, and to put myself in the best defensive position depending on the pitcher's pitch. He emphasized that I should divide my efforts as I ran the bases to find the ball and the outfielder, hoping to take an extra base.

But I had also learned that even if I was the best of the best, if I didn't surround myself with people who would help build my character, it would all be for nothing. Baseball is a team game, and every team is only as strong as its weakest link. I would never get anywhere if I didn't surround myself with the right people who would build me up and whom I could consider friends and family.

One evening, I visited Mr. Davis to share my thoughts and thank him for what he did. I was wondering if I could put into words my respect and affection for him. When I arrived, I saw the old man sitting on the porch with a baseball glove and a cup of coffee in the other.

"Jack, my boy!" Mr. Davis exclaimed with a smile as he saw me approaching. "How's the season been treating you?"

"Not bad, sir. Not bad."

And with that, I started telling him everything I had experienced, as if he had never attended the games or been seen walking around while I was training with the team. And he listened attentively as if it were the world's most important story, and if only he and I existed at that moment.

I told him things he already knew — like how I felt the first time I attended training with my nerves rattling through my body. I laughingly told him how I worried the bat would slip out of my hands or the ball would fall out of my glove like it did at the beginning of the summer.

Mr. Davis laughed, never commenting, as if he wanted to soak it in before saying anything. It was the first time I saw the smile reach his eyes, and I felt proud that it was because of me. That old man had changed my life forever, and I could only repay him by making him proud of the person I was becoming.

With all the good feelings we were sharing, I didn't want to sour the mood by saying something negative. But I owed it to my mentor to mention that dark side of baseball for me:

"At some point, it all got too much for me to handle, Mr. Davis."

He looked at me with a hint of understanding but said nothing again.

"One day, I went back to the sandlot where I met Taylor, one of my buddies, and I told him about this. I explained how much I missed the fun of the summer's plays, the jokes, and the pranks in the middle of a game. And do you know what he told me, Mr. Davis? You won't believe it. He told me that there's more to life than just baseball!"

Again, he laughed. This time, I started laughing, too, because I knew he agreed with me. There were more things besides baseball in life, obviously. Still, baseball was at the pinnacle of my top three.

"It is because there is more to life than just baseball, young man," he said.

"I know, sir! But baseball is one of the most important things for me, I love the game and I love the way playing the game makes me feel!"

"I completely understand, Jack. But your friend Taylor is right; baseball is just the vehicle, and you don't love a bicycle or a car above the people you carry with you, right? You care about the destination and getting there with the ones you love. But if the vehicle breaks down at some point, the first thing you will worry about is not the car's condition but that of the people traveling with you. If the car breaks down, it will delay your plans, and you may even have to change your destination or make stops along the way that were outside the planned route. But that doesn't mean you will stop moving forever; you must adapt to the changes. It's the same with baseball."

"I don't understand, sir. What do you mean? That baseball is not important?" I was about to freak out. It sounded like Mr. Davis, the Major League All-Star player, George Davis, my mentor, was minimizing baseball!

"Breathe, kiddo. It's not that baseball is not important; it's only that there are more important things than the game."

The most important lesson I would ever receive came as I recovered from the shock.

"You have made me proud, Jack, so proud. I have seen you giving all you got to make your dreams come true. But now you need to learn that baseball, as such, is just a game. However, as time passes and you understand it better, you will see that it has stopped being just a game and become something worth playing for; it has become a metaphor for life. The challenges we face on the field, the difficulties, and the victories and defeats are the same as in life. They're all part of the journey. Fortunately, or unfortunately, life is about falling and getting up. And the lessons we learn from each one of the falls can help us become better people, both on and off the field."

"Then… that means at some point baseball will stop being a game for me?" I asked.

"No, Jack. I hope that day never comes. It only means that, at some point, you will realize that even if you are losing, you can allow yourself to have fun playing the game."

Now I know that there are hundreds of ways to get you wherever you want to go — hundreds of ways that will lead you to places you didn't know even existed and hundreds that will lead you to places you never wanted to go to the first place. In those ways, the most critical part is treasuring the people accompanying you as you enjoy the journey and have fun. It was never about the destination; it was all about the road getting there.

As the sun began to dip below the horizon, Mr. Davis shared stories of his experiences as a professional baseball player: The friendships he had made, the obstacles he had overcome, and the wisdom he had gained along the way. I listened closely, captivated by Mr. Davis's tales and the insights they offered.

As the evening drew close and it was time for me to go home, Mr. Davis placed a hand on my shoulder and looked me in the eye.

"Remember, Jack," he said, "no matter where life takes you or how high you soar, always stay grounded and true to yourself. Cherish the memories, learn from the challenges, and never forget the passion for the game that brought you here. Remember the love of those who believed in you even in your darkest times; stay true to them. Hear me, son. I cannot assure you that you will have an easy life, but I can assure you that every time you face a problem, you'll have the strength and support to overcome it."

I was just a child and couldn't fully understand the depth of Mr. Davis's words. Only when I grew up and faced the different problems that life put in front of me would I become aware of their true meaning? If I stayed true to myself and those who loved me, any obstacle could be considered small in comparison.

As Mr. Davis told me, I kept company with the people who rejoiced for me on the happiest days and accompanied me in the silence of the saddest ones. They have made the journey worth enjoying.

CHAPTER 7

Dreams Take Flight

The first day of high school baseball tryouts also happened to be my 15th birthday. My mom said it was a sign that I was destined to make the varsity. Privately, I thought it might be a sign that I was going to vomit up birthday cake if I wound up getting cut. I had been one of the top junior players for the last two years and was named league MVP. But now I had my sights set on finding a spot in my high school's baseball program. Baseball was immensely popular and just about every kid played. That meant that the program was stacked with kids - varsity, junior high, a sophomore team, and a Freshman A and Freshman B squad as well. Easily more than 100 boys in the program. Most guys my age would wind up on the freshman teams. The A team was for guys who looked decent enough that the coaches wanted to see them playing every day against competition at their own level and start charting a course for them through the program so they could contribute on varsity as juniors and seniors. The B team was for the guys whose bodies hadn't hit the big growth spurt yet, or maybe their dads knew the coaches really well and wanted them to have a spot on the team somewhere. The sophomore team usually had a few freshmen on it - guys who had been playing a while and weren't quite ready for the big time but would be wasted on the Freshman teams. If you had been crushing it in the Junior League, you were going to eat other teams' freshman pitchers alive. If you were a freshman on a team of sophomores, it meant you were on the fast track to get to the varsity at some point in your sophomore year. That was the spot I was angling for. I knew most of the guys by name or reputation that were trying out with me, and I knew that very few of them, if any, were up to my level. I wanted to show out in the field, at the plate, and on the basepaths and prove that I was one of the future stars of the Willow Creek Warriors.

About the only thing bringing clouds to this sunny day was the fact that Jimmy Pearson was also trying out that day. I had not seen Jimmy much since we won the title together years ago on his famous bunt double and my title-winning home run. He lived on the opposite side of town, and he was always playing with a traveling team. I had been recruited by several of those teams, which went all over California and sometimes to tournaments in Colorado, Arizona, and other states to compete against other all-star teams, but they were really expensive. Even when the coaches tried to bend my ear and tell me they could give my family a 25% or 50% discount on the costs, I said no without even asking my mom and dad. I knew they couldn't afford it and didn't want to make them feel bad for having to admit it. So, while I was dominating the Junior League, Jimmy was gone with his squad for almost the entire summer showing off his talents all over the West Coast.

By the start of my freshman year of high school, I had sprouted to about 5 feet 10 inches and weighed in at 170 pounds. I had muscular arms and legs but didn't look like I was lifting weights all day long. My muscles had developed from relentless training - running the bases, batting practice, and chasing down fly balls. My hair had gone blonde from so much time in the sun, and I had a year-round tan. I was mistaken for an older player a lot, because of how tall I had grown and from the way I hit the ball. I have to admit, I loved it when it happened. It made me feel like my play was making people really notice me.

Jimmy, on the other hand, looked like he could have been 35 years old by the time he showed up for the first day of tryouts. He was 15 but now stood 6'4" with a huge chest and powerful shoulders. He was a little on the stout side throughout his middle and his legs looked like tree trunks. He wasn't going to be stealing 30 bases a year anytime soon, but the kind of power that he was able to generate meant he'd be trotting around the bases a lot on long home runs.

Jimmy had never gotten over not being the big hero that day years ago, even those his double had thrown the opposition off and kept the game alive so I could bat. I got interviewed after the game and spent a long time talking up his contribution, but all my praise hadn't made the story in the paper, and it was my picture, not his, on the front page.

From what I heard from friends who played on his teams, he had been clobbering the ball for the past three years like it had my face painted on it. When he got around on balls, he destroyed them. He had even had his name mentioned in a little blurb in a national sports magazine after having a 5-game stretch at a regional tournament where he hit 7 home runs and drove in 16. When Jimmy got into the batting cage at the tryouts, you could hear a lot of buzz pick up and it seemed like even the varsity coaches were coming closer to see what he was going to do.

He didn't disappoint his audience. The first seven swings he took all cleared the fence. He hit the ball to all fields and the guys in the infield who used batting practice to take reps at their positions started to get bored - every ball was flying at least 350 feet! When Jimmy finally hit one lower, the third baseman ducked in terror as it came to him like a laser beam. I lost count of how many home runs Jimmy hit before his time in the cage was done, but it earned him applause from the players gathered around him.

In my earlier days, I would have been very tempted to try to match Jimmy's power performance when my turn in the cage came, but I knew that wasn't playing to my strengths. I hit a good share of home runs, but it wasn't the strength of my game. I hit the ball hard on a line down the first and third-base lines, or into the outfield gaps. I was the kind of guy who could turn a routine single into a double if the outfielders weren't taking me seriously, and I was always looking for the advantage to turn a double into a triple. I settled into the batter's box and did what I did best, spraying the ball to all fields. I knocked a few over the fence, including one to dead center field that earned more than a few whistles. I couldn't match Jimmy's raw power, but I thought it was about the best showcase I could have done for the coaches.

The next day-and-a-half saw us go through the paces for the high school coaches. I stretched, I ran, I took fly balls, I hit the cutoff man, I stole bases, I avoided getting picked off, and I went through a ton of situational exercises to see how smart I was in terms of baseball IQ. I wish Mr. Davis could have seen it all, because he would have loved the way we worked. It was the kind of mental baseball he had been teaching to me for a long time. But the tryouts were closed to parents and anyone else, so the players didn't have to have their parents or other adults hollering at them and making a high-pressure situation even worse.

On Friday afternoon at 3 p.m., the program's head coach - Melvin Cerny - was going to post the rosters of all the program's teams for the year. That meant that every single player in the program would be out there to check out where they were headed. The seniors who had played varsity a year before had nothing to worry about, but they would come out anyway just to make sure they were safe and to see who their new teammates would be. For juniors and sophomores, it was nerve-racking to see if you had done enough to get moved up to the next level - if you had been a freshman on the sophomore team and didn't get moved up to at least junior varsity, it was a real blow to your confidence.

For all of us freshmen, the fear was the most pronounced. We hoped to be on the sophomore squad, but nearly all of us would be on one of the freshman rosters. Or even worse, if you had struggled at the tryouts and you were a ninth grader, your name might not show up at all, meaning you didn't even rate the Freshman B team and wouldn't be playing for the school. If you didn't think you did well, there was the temptation to not be there when the rosters were revealed and just sneak out to see later on when the crowd had died down. But if you were a competitor, you usually were too tough to take the easy way out.

The crowd of players around Coach Cerny's office was already pushing triple digits when I showed up after my last class. My Spanish class was on the other side of campus, and I didn't' want to seem like a dork by running all the way to the PE offices, even though that's what I felt like doing. Coach Cerny's office door was closed, which meant he hadn't revealed anything yet. The only rule after he posted the lists was that nobody or their parents were allowed in his office until the following Monday. He wanted everyone to have time to think about where they were assigned before they started complaining.

We all stood there making idle chatter, whispering things to those closest to us, but mostly just trying to mentally will his door to open. When it finally did, his assistant coach, Tom McPherson, had to threaten us all with extra laps to make space by the bulletin board. Coach Cerny posted one list after another from varsity on down. He turned, thanked us all for our efforts, and told us to have a good weekend.

As soon as he stepped away, the floodgates opened. Everyone pushed forward to find their name. Everyone was jabbering at once as they put their hands on one list or another to unveil the truth. Big as a tree, Jimmy pulled his way through the crowd of smaller players and his big hand landed on the sophomore list. He squinted at it and traced one beefy finger down the list of typed names. Then stopped and tapped the board once, pumping his fist as a big grin came on his face.

"Sophomore!" he called out, and several of the other boys gave him praise for it. It was to be expected. His power stroke was uncommon, even in a state as baseball crazy as California. If he worked hard, they might call him up to the varsity for a taste when the rosters got expanded for the playoffs.

A gap opened up where Jimmy had been, and I was one of a few guys to fill it. I raced my index finger down the sophomore list, got to the end, reversed course, and came to the bitter truth. I wasn't on the team. Something in my stomach made a flopping sensation, and suddenly I was that little misfit back on the edge of the sandlot, trying so hard to be noticed but falling short. It was my first setback on the baseball field in a long time, and I didn't like it one bit. I thought I had been a lock for the sophomore squad, but maybe there were just too many guys from last year's freshman squad that were ahead of me. Regardless, I vowed to show Coach Cerny every day that I was worth more and needed to move up quickly.

As I moved my hand away from the list, I heard a low chuckle behind me and turned to see Jimmy standing over me with a nasty look on his face.

"Tough break, Thompson," he said with a sneer. "Looks like you're going to be in the baby pool this season. Tell you what, if you want to carry my bag after the game, maybe I'll give you an autograph, yeah?"

It took a lot not to say anything, and even more so not to take a swing at him. But that was a surefire way to get on Coach Cerny's bad side right away, not to mention that Jimmy probably outweighed me by 100 pounds and had 6 inches of height on me. I couldn't play on any team with my face caved in.

I turned away with an effort and moved to the Freshman A team to see who my teammates would be this season. That was the silver lining of not making the sophomore squad, I'd be playing with guys all my age, most of whom I had a good relationship with from various summer and club leagues.

I smiled several times at the familiar names I saw on the list. We were definitely going to have some fun and be a pretty competitive team as well. Then I paused. Something was off. I read the list of names again. It was missing one very important one: Jack Thompson.

My heart started pounding. It had to be a mistake! I hadn't even made the Freshman A team. How was that possible? I had been an All-Star at every level the past few years and I had excelled throughout the tryouts. Was it something personal? Did I make someone mad without realizing it? Was it because my parents weren't American? I couldn't believe I would have to start my high school career at the bottom of the totem pole on Freshman B. It was embarrassing and painful and …

I did a double take. I wasn't on the B roster either. I had been cut from the program altogether.

I lost it. I knew the rule about not going into the coach's office to question their decisions until Monday, but this was outrageous. How dare they! How dare they run me out of the program!

Coach Cerny and his assistant were just a few feet inside the office when I busted in, and both turned to me with raised eyebrows.

"I get that maybe I'm not ready for sophomores, but where do you get off not putting me on either freshman team?!" I half yelled; half sobbed. I was way too emotional, and I didn't care. "I've been an All-Star for the last four years! Why are you doing this to me?"

The two coaches exchanged glances and then Coach McPherson said, "You're right, Jack. We don't think you belong on either freshman team, or with the sophomores, either."

I slammed my hand down on the coach's desk, startling several of the players still staring at the lists posted outside. I realized I was making a scene, and everyone was watching, but I didn't care.

"This doesn't make any sense!" I cried. "What did I ever do to you?"

Coach Cerny walked towards me and for one terrible moment I thought he was going to slap me in the face out of insolence. Instead, he put his hand on my shoulder and turned me around, moving me out of his office.

"Come here, son, I need to show you something," he said softly.

I followed him out, feeling humiliated as every other guy there stared at me, probably wanting to see what my punishment could be.

Instead, Coach Cerny led me down to the far end of the bulletin board and pointed at the first list on the wall.

There, at the very end of the column of names, it read "Jack Thompson, Freshman."

He tapped it twice for emphasis as I gaped wide-eyed down at my name then back up to the top of the list.

I had made the varsity.

* * * * *

It was March of my sophomore year, and I was out after practice taking some extra hitting sessions with a couple of my buddies on the team. Billy Harrison was a junior who was trying to be our starting second baseman and Mikey Plummer was a barrel-chested pitcher who was a senior who played some third base and pitched a bit as well. The three of us were an unlikely trio in that we were all in different years at school, but we all had the same interests - which included baseball, baseball, and you guessed it, more baseball. We had decided to do extra work a couple of times a week together to make sure we were all in the lineup when the district season started.

I didn't want to get a big head, but I knew the centerfield job was already mine. I had started the last 27 games of my freshman year and ended up playing in 35 of the team's 40 games overall. I hit .321, the third-highest average on the team and stole 27 bases. The coaches were excited about my progress, and they had already talked to me about moving up to the leadoff spot in the lineup. I had worked hard all summer on my bunting and base-stealing skills. Mr. Davis had met me more than a few times to talk about the nuances of both and I was excited to get out there and test my talents against real, live talent.

The only problem with practicing with Billy and Mikey is that Mikey had recently started dating a girl named Deena Jones, and because they were suddenly so madly in love, she made the habit of being wherever he was, all the time. That meant she was sitting in the bleachers clapping every time he did anything remotely exciting and called his name and yelled "Whoa!" a lot. It was OK at first, but about a week into that, she had been joined by her younger sister, Michelle, who was a junior. Michelle came and sat next to Deena and the two of them talked and laughed and hollered at us and told us about a good job while we worked out. When we got done and went to the locker room to get cleaned up, Michelle raised her hand, smiled awkwardly, and said, "Oh, hi Jack!"

I mumbled "Hi" back, too tired for a conversation, and headed off to get cleaned up. A couple of days later, the crowd was Deena, Michelle, and three or four of her friends, also juniors. Now they were all giggling and laughing and clapping their hands. Every time we came off the field and Mikey went to talk to Deena and get heaps of compliments, Michelle would wave at me and say "Hi, Jack." Except now that was accompanied by scores of giggles from her friends. I couldn't figure out what their deal was. None of them seemed to know the first thing about baseball, so why were they out there? Maybe Deena was giving them all a ride home? It felt a lot like they were making fun of us, so I tried not to worry about it.

One afternoon, Billy was sick, and Mikey had a date with Deena, so it was just me out there. It's hard to practice baseball at a high level by yourself, but I made due with a batting tee and some basic drills. When I went to get cleaned up in the clubhouse, I was surprised to find Coach Cerny was there in his office, wearing reading glasses, going over lineup schemes.

"Jack!" he said with a smile. "Thought I was the only one working late."

I smiled back. "No sir, I always have stuff I can improve on if I want to be the best."

"Good man," he replied, looking at me over the top of his glasses. "Say, Jack, are you free Saturday morning? I'd like to talk to you about something, pick your brain on it."

"Of course, Coach!" I exclaimed, excited at the possibilities of 1:1 time with my high school coach. "I'll be here early!"

On Saturday morning, I was supposed to meet Coach Cerny at 6 a.m. at the field. When I got there, wearing my tennis shoes, athletic shorts, a T-shirt, and my cap, I was surprised to find that he was decidedly not dressed for baseball.

He was wearing a camouflage vest, baggy brown pants, boots, and floppy hat covered in hooks.

He looked at me and laughed, "No baseball today, Jack! I want you to come fishing with me!"

Fishing? Was he serious? The season started in three weeks, and he wanted to go sit in a boat on a lake staring at nothing for hours on end? I thought maybe it was a test so I tried to fake as much enthusiasm as I could.

"Oh, yeah, fishing! Sounds great, Coach. Um, let me put my glove in my locker, OK?"

He grinned at me, clearly seeing that I wasn't very excited about the change of plans.

An hour later, we were doing exactly what I feared we'd be doing. Sitting in a small boat in the middle of a lake staring at nothing, doing nothing, while no fish bit our lines. I wondered if Coach Cerny knew how much he was torturing me.

After at least 20 minutes without saying a word, Coach Cerny let out a slow breath and said, "Jack, let me ask you a question, what do you like doing with your life besides baseball?"

What kind of question was that? Why would my baseball coach want to know what I liked doing besides baseball? Me being obsessed with baseball made his job that much easier. He didn't have to motivate me; I was doing that for myself 24 hours a day.

"Uhhh, I like to read, Coach," I managed to get out.

"Oh really? What subjects do you like?"

"Umm, you know, books about, well, baseball and famous baseball players," I sheepishly responded.

"So that's it? Just baseball?"

JUST BASEBALL? His talk reminded me of what Mr. Davis had said about some things being more important than baseball. I really couldn't figure out where the conversation was going.

"Um, Coach Cerny, I don't mean to sound rude, but what's this all about?"

He turned around to face me in the boat.

"Jack, you know my wife, right? Cindy Cerny? Teaches home economics?"

I nodded. I hadn't taken the class but knew what and where it was.

"Well Jack, my wife has a lot of busybodies in her class, like Michelle Jones, who would rather gossip than learn the basics. That's OK, because she doesn't mind it, but they seem to be focused on one subject all the time, any idea what it is?"

I shrugged my shoulders. I had no idea where this was going, and I was feeling dumber by the minute.

Coach Cerny leaned closer and looked me straight in the eyes.

"The thing that Michelle and her friends are always gossiping about is a star baseball player named Jack Thompson. They talked about what he wore to school today. They talk about seeing him smile in the cafeteria. They talk about how cute he looked when he got all sweaty in gym class. They talk about how they think he got even cuter over Winter Break or how he wore a tight shirt, and you could really see his biceps through it. They talk about how Michelle says hi to him every day after baseball, but he just doesn't seem to get the message."

"What, they talk about me all the time? What for?"

Coach Cerny looked like he was ready to throw me overboard and call it a day.

"Because she likes you, genius. Because she thinks you're handsome. Because she would probably give up sleepovers and makeup and washing her hair for a year if it meant going on a date with you sometime."

"Me ... me?" I stuttered out. "Michelle Jones likes me?

"He's finally figured it out, ladies and gentlemen! Yes, dear boy, she likes you. Girls don't usually watch two hours of three guys practicing baseball just to say 'hi' for two seconds if they don't have an obvious crush on one of them."

The revelation hit me like a ton of bricks, or a 95-mile-per-hour fastball to the middle of the shoulder blades. I had no idea that any girl liked me, much less that they were talking about me! Michelle was really pretty. I had seen her enough to know that, and I noticed plenty of girls, but I had been painfully shy around them. Guys that knew how to talk to a girl or make her laugh or get her phone number seemed like an alien species to me. I just kept putting baseball first and hoped that figuring out girls would come to me at some point, although I was 16 and it hadn't so far. I couldn't believe she was coming to our little practices every day just to see me.

I realized Coach Cerny was still staring at me.

"So, what should I do?" I asked, realizing how dumb it sounded as I said it.

"For goodness' sake, Jack, figure it out!" he hollered, scaring a few nearby birds into flight. "When she says hi to you next time, say hi back and ask her if she wants to go out for a milkshake with you."

"A milkshake? Coach, I don't know, that's a lot of calories right after a workout, I don't think that's a great idea for ---"

He cut me off with a look.

"You don't have to drink the entire milkshake, Jack. You can take one sip for all I care. The point is that the girl likes you and you need to have more of a life than stolen bases and leading off first. Have some fun. Meet a new person. See if there's a connection. Talk about literally anything besides baseball. Ask her about herself. Stop being so one-tracked. Look around you kid, it's a big, beautiful world and it goes way beyond the centerfield fence."

I couldn't concentrate that next Monday during our three-man practice. I kept looking up into the stands where Michelle and her sister and her friend sat. Michelle was a year older than me and seemed way more mature, but unless she and Coach Cerny and everyone else were in on a big joke, she clearly was coming out to watch me practice and that meant something. Today, she was wearing a bright yellow dress and had her hair pulled back with a yellow flower tucked behind one ear. I'd be lying if I said I didn't have a lot of daydreams that year that started with seeing her in that dress.

Practice seemed to race by yet also take a long time to get done. I swung and missed at pitches I always hit, dropped a pop up that I could have caught when I was 10, and nearly took Mikey's head off with an errant throw.

When we called it quits, we headed for the clubhouse and Mikey went to talk to Deena. Right on cue, Michelle raised her hand to me and waved, saying "Hi Jack!" with a little smile.

Despite being absolutely terrified of what would come next, I raised my hand back to her, smiled and said, "Hi, Michelle."

She did a double take. I can't say I blamed her. I had barely spoken to her in all the times she had come out. She seemed even more surprised when I walked straight up to her, her friends frantically whispering as I did.

I stopped about three feet from her, thankful that I was a workaholic when it came to preparation and had practiced my lines for this well into the early hours of the morning.

"Hi," I said again. "I wanted to say thanks for coming out to watch us practice all these days. That's really nice of you."

"Oh," she responded, tripping over her own words a little, which made me a lot less nervous for some reason. "Oh, of course. Well, my sister is dating Mikey, and you know, I thought it would be fun to watch and hang out with her." She smiled and tucked her hair behind her ear.

This was it. I was nervous beyond belief, but the thought of Coach Cerny finding out I had blown my assignment was even more frightening.

"Why don't you let me thank you for all your support?" I stammered out. "Would you like to go get a milkshake with me and hang out?"

I mentally prepared for the rejection, but it never came. Instead, she was nodding furiously, her eyes shiny and clear.

"I'd like that very much, Jack. Very much indeed."

* * * * *

It was a normal Wednesday evening. Nothing particularly unusual was taking place. The weather was getting milder as the chilly days of winter faded into history. Walking down the street during these days was most pleasing, with that cooling breeze occasionally interrupted by the warmth of the sun's rays. It could have been an ordinary afternoon, like all the others. But something extraordinary was about to happen.

I had been training with the baseball team, so coming home meant a sweet rest. I took a shower and tackled the homework waiting for me. By the time my parents arrived, I had already finished, and I entertained myself by watching TV for a while.

An ordinary day… until I heard my father excitedly calling my name.

"Jack, son," my father called from the kitchen. "There's a letter for you!"

"A letter, Dad? From who?"

"It's from the University of Southern California. That's an expensive one indeed," he said hesitantly.

I thought he was joking until he showed me the envelope and I saw the school's insignia.

"We told you, Jack," Dad said, sounding somber. "We are so sorry, but we can't afford to send you to this institution. We understand that you wanted to try and apply just to see if you would have gotten into the school, but…."

"Oh no, Dad. I never sent an application to this University; I have no idea what's going on."

I still remember the sadness in their eyes, a lifetime of work, blood, sweat, and tears for over a decade, and still, they could only afford to send me to a public university when the time came. We had lost years to their work; there was a time when we didn't even see each other on Sundays. It had all been work for them and the frustration of not being able to attend most of my games during my high school years. I saw the despair in their eyes at the thought that I might have sent an application to a university like USC.

But I knew the reality at home and would never have put them in that position. "I promise you, Dad. I didn't apply to this school."

I had big dreams, but I wasn't about to take my family down financially to fulfill them. It would have been useless for me to achieve greatness on the field if my family suffered. Baseball made me extremely happy, but only because they were there to see and encourage me.

My mom took the letter out of my dad's hands, unable to contain her anticipation, and opened it. She was the bravest of us three that evening. My dad and I were stuck looking at the envelope, trying to figure out what it was all about without opening it.

As she read it, her face went from a golden hue to the whitest of whites and then to the broadest smile I had ever seen on her face. She started to shout and jump and hug me and Dad all at the same time.

"Oh, my God! Oh my God, Jack! The University of Southern California just offered you a full academic and athletic scholarship!"

They did what? I thought. That was impossible.

"Look, honey!" Mom said to Dad. "Our son got a full scholarship to one of the best universities in the country! Oh my, Jack, I'm so proud of you!"

After that, everything happened so fast. My dad took the letter from her hands and started reading while she was still squeezing me. From his face, I wasn't sure if he was happy or about to faint. He grabbed the counter to steady himself and looked at me like I was a stranger in his house. How was his son, who was never a little league starter, let alone an all-star, getting a letter from a nationally ranked college baseball powerhouse? That day would change his life as much as it changed mine. I still don't know how I didn't think it was a joke.

I spent the next few days in shock, unable to believe my dream was coming true. But it was true.

And I owed it all to that little sandlot and Mr. Davis.

I visited the sandlot often those days, just as a reminder of where it all began.

When Michelle and I had started dating, I had taken her on a picnic there and slowly explained the entire story to her of how it had shaped my life. For quite a while, she thought I was pulling her leg, and I guess I can see why. By the time we started going out together, I was an All-Star center fielder starting on the varsity squad as a sophomore.

Thinking of me as a clumsy kid with no coordination who couldn't catch a popup five years ago seemed pretty implausible. Michelle and I dated for almost a year before we broke things off amicably. Since she was a year ahead of me at school, her senior year ended and she got accepted to Georgetown University in Washington, D.C. She was hoping to be a lawyer one day. We were young and naive, but we both knew that an East Coast / West Coast relationship where one person was in college and the other was in high school just wasn't going to work. I took her to her senior prom, danced about 30 slow dances with her, and kissed her until her dad came outside and banged on the hood of the car a few times to get the point across that the date was over. We had exchanged letters for a while, and I saw her when she came home for Christmas and Spring Break. We had turned from first loves to good friends and I was grateful for it. Even though it was expensive, I called her long-distance that night in D.C. to tell her the good news. She squealed with delight and told me how proud she was of me, and made plans to come see a game the following spring in Los Angeles.

Most of my teammates and friends were more jealous of the co-ed situation at USC than me playing baseball there. The campus was famous for its beautiful California girls, and I was not averse to meeting them, although I already knew that my main focuses were going to be dominating on the diamond and meeting expectations on the field. I still wasn't crazy about school, but doing well in the classroom was the only way to stay eligible on the field in college. I figured I'd have plenty of time for love, dating, and romance if I made it to the Major Leagues, or whatever happened next. But at the time baseball still felt like a full-time job.

My friends thought I was insane because of my priorities, of course. Right after Michelle and I started going out when I was a sophomore, a bunch of girls, some I knew and some I didn't, got all in a huff that

I was dating someone. They told me, my friends, and anyone who would listen that if they had known that I was single, THEY would have asked me out first. I made a joke to a few of them that I hadn't realized that I had to declare myself single like declaring for the MLB amateur draft, but nobody got my obscure baseball humor. After Michelle and I broke up, I went to a few movies with girls, a couple of parties, and took a really cute girl named Katherine to the homecoming dance, but none of those dates panned out into anything more significant. It wasn't that I was stuck up or picky or anything like that, I just knew that once baseball season came, I'd be locked in and would be a terrible boyfriend. Once baseball season was over, I'd be preparing to play at whatever college offered me the best deal and wouldn't want to start a relationship just to turn around and end it.

My transparent approach to dating didn't exactly win me a lot of friends, but at least I was being honest.

I hit .379 my sophomore year and made the All-City first team as the Warriors won the division and made it to the second round of the playoffs.

As a junior, I moved from leadoff to batting third as I got more power in my body. I played every single inning of every single game that year, and led us to not only another district title, but the regional crown as well. It was the deepest that Willow Creek High School had made it into the playoffs since before World War II. I hit .412 for the season, a new school record for a junior, and added 11 home runs and 37 stolen bases in 50 games. I also led the team in runs scored, RBI, doubles, triples, and walks. The only category I wasn't at the top of was home runs. Despite our early differences, Jimmy Pearson and I had turned into the most lethal 1-2 combination in Northern California high school baseball. He hit 24 home runs as a junior, and signed with Arizona State before our senior season began.

As our swan song to high school, Jimmy and I led the team to the state semifinals before we bowed out in a 2-1 12-inning thriller. The other team ensured that neither one of us would beat them, walking us each intentionally 3 times. With Jimmy a base ahead of me every time, I couldn't steal, and my speed was neutralized. We left it all on the field though, and that's all you can ask for. I hit .459 for the year with 17 home runs, 68 RBI, and 47 stolen bases. I was named first-team All-State center fielder. Jimmy hit 33 home runs, a new California state record. We split Player of the Year honors. I can't say we were ever truly friends, but we destroyed a lot of pitching staffs together, and were photographed together for a lot of newspaper articles.

As I prepared for the next chapter of my life, I wanted to ensure every memory was tucked safely away in my mind. The challenges ahead would be more significant than ever and being away from home only made them seem bigger and bigger. It was the first time I would ever leave the safe, calm embrace of Willow Creek for more than a couple of days.

I was terrified. Totally and utterly terrified.

All the doubts that plagued me rose to the surface. Every one of my insecurities whispered in my ear that it couldn't be true. I had never achieved anything without pushing myself to the limits of the impossible. That scholarship seemed like a gift from heaven. I would be competing against the best players in the country, all vying for a chance to make it to the major leagues. And as strange as it sounds, despite all that, in the back of my mind, it was clear to me that all the lessons I had learned from Mr. Davis, from my friends, from my parents, from my experience on and off the field had prepared me for that exact future.

Before I knew it, I found myself standing at the precipice of high school graduation. It was a time of reflection, a moment to ponder upon the countless hours I had invested in pursuing excellence both on and off the field. With each passing day, baseball had etched its mark on my soul, shaping the person I aspired to become.

From the early days of my youth, the diamond had been my sanctuary. Within those chalked lines, I discovered the essence of who I truly was. The sport demanded my dedication, my unwavering commitment, and I embraced it wholeheartedly. The passion to excel coursed through my veins, never waning, never dimming.

As I toiled relentlessly, a gradual transformation occurred. Bit by bit, I carved out a niche for myself on the high school baseball team. The journey was arduous, filled with challenges and setbacks, but I refused to succumb to the self-doubt that was always there to try and take it all away. Every failure became an opportunity to learn, grow, and push myself further.

Slowly but surely, my prowess on the diamond had begun to resonate beyond the confines of our small town. News of my exploits spread like wildfire throughout the area. The whispers of my name carried the weight of my dedication and determination. It was a reputation I had unknowingly forged that caught the attention of college coaches converging on Willow Creek to watch me play.

It's important to understand the magnitude of this attention. Few high school baseball players ever capture the notice of college coaches, let alone those from NCAA Division I schools. The odds were stacked against me from the start. I was competing against a sea of talent, players who had honed their skills and shared the same dream I did.

Suddenly, my dreams seemed within reach. The thought of playing baseball at the college level ignited a fire within me. The college coaches' interest validated my sacrifices, the countless hours of practice, and honing my skills. Every throw, every swing of the bat, became a test, a chance to prove that I was part of the elite.

As the college coaches observed me, I knew this was my chance to prove myself and demonstrate the depths of my passion and potential. I stepped onto the field with a renewed sense of purpose; every swing of the bat and every throw was my audition for the next level. It was my time to shine, and I was determined to leave an indelible mark on the minds of those who watched.

One spring evening, as the sun descended beyond the horizon, I found myself at home, enveloped in the bittersweet embrace of the end of my senior year. It was a time of transition, a juncture where the threads of my past were interwoven with the anticipation of an uncertain future. As the weight of reality settled upon my shoulders, I experienced a whirlwind of emotions, oscillating between excitement and trepidation.

I felt a strange electric surge, the tingling sensation that dances across your skin when you suddenly grasp the enormity of your life's potential. A storm had erupted within me, causing my body to shiver and my feet to turn icy cold. As I sat there, contemplative, and reflective, the realization struck me with great force. Graduation was speeding ever closer, and with it came the undeniable truth that in my life that I would have some big decisions to make. Gone was the safety of the familiar hallways, the regular rhythms of high school, the comfort of the sandlot, and the warmth of home and family — they were all about to fade into distant memories. At that moment, I was caught between two worlds.

Little did I know then that the shivers and cold feet were not signs of weakness but rather reminders of the sheer magnitude of the transformation unfolding before me. In those seemingly ordinary moments sitting in my home, I was preparing to embrace the future, whatever it may be.

*****

I struck out 10 straight times to open my career at USC.

Oh, not all in three or four games, mind you, that would have driven me to drinking, or something worse. But the first 10 times I got in a game in the first half of my freshman year, I struck out. My first few times up were as a pinch hitter in garbage time of big wins or blowout losses. The first few were late in games that had already been decided. I got a few good cuts, hit some hard foul balls, but I still struck out each time. In the third week of the season, I saw my name in the starting lineup for the first time. I was excited, but not overwhelmed, because our starting center fielder had missed practice the day before after being too drunk to set his alarm the night before. My coach at USC, Robert Clark, had a zero tolerance policy for unexcused absences or failing grades. So not only did he not let the hungover junior play, but he let the darn freshman hot shot take his spot. It was a chance to prove myself early, but all I did was prove I was too eager. I was 0-for-4 with 4 strikeouts in a 16-3 victory. Everyone else in the lineup got at least one hit and scored at least one run except for me. I did make a really nice over-the-shoulder catch at one point, but nobody cares about a defensive gem when you win by 13 runs.

My strikeout streak finally broke on February 21st. It was a Tuesday and I had gone to the cage early to try and sort myself out. Coach Clark was there helping one of our pitchers work on his finger positioning to throw a knuckle curve and after a few minutes he walked over to watch me hit (or try to).

I was being aggressive and trying to murder every pitch when Coach Clark gave a low whistle and I looked up in surprise.

"Jack," he said. "What did you bat last year at Willow Creek?"

I made a show of thinking about it, even though I really didn't have to. I loved baseball stats, and my own were emblazoned in my mind forever.

"Um, around .459, Coach."

"And the year before that?"

".412, sir."

"Not bad, not bad at all. But here's the problem, Jack. Those two guys that hit over .400. They're not here anymore. They retired back in high school. Jack Thompson, all-state center fielder, doesn't go to USC. Just Jack, aspiring freshman student athlete. He's the guy I'm waiting to see show up in my lineup."

I really wanted to know what Coach Clark was talking about, but it was over my head. Thankfully, he was a patient guy.

"You came in here expecting to be the great hitter that you were a year ago, Jack. You're not that guy. This is the PAC-10 and every guy you are going to face here was Mr. Baseball at his school and earned a scholarship just like you. Stop being the high school all-star and remember what it's like to be a ballplayer whose only mission in life is to put good metal on the ball and drive it hard at a spot on the field where nobody can catch it. Got me, rook?"

I nodded. He was right. I was playing like I belonged among the elite of the team instead of working my way up the ladder. I had to start over and figure out how the college game was played.

Coach Clark decided to test my understanding immediately. When I headed over to the stadium that day, my name was in the starting lineup and I was batting leadoff.

I heard some grumbling up and down the dugout as a result, but I knew I couldn't let it get to me. Just like every other team I had ever played for, actions always spoke louder than words.

After an 0-for-10 start, I went 4-for-4 after my talk with Coach Clark. After taking two strikes in the top of the first inning, I dropped a drag bunt down the third-base line and beat the throw to the bag for my first hit as a Trojan. On the second pitch after that, I took off and stole second base with a headfirst slide. The other team's pitcher didn't bother calling timeout while he tried to get dirt out of one of his cleats. While his back was turned to me, I raced to third without a throw. Two stolen bags in one pitch. Jack Thompson, USC Trojan, was making quite a name for himself.

The college years proved to be both challenging and rewarding. I dedicated myself to my studies and baseball; everything else was out of my mind. I saw my friend's attending parties and heard them talking about the girls they had met. Still, I needed to be more focused on maintaining that scholarship. Soon, all my efforts paid me back in spades. I became a starter at Southern Cal during the second half of my freshman year. From the start, I knew I was meant to shine on the baseball field. My position as a center fielder was to the best utilization of my skills and allowed me to be the spirit of the team. I always tried to be more than just another player; I always strived to be the motor, heart, and soul that held us together.

In the lineup, I was a rare breed, a power hitter with exceptional speed and arm strength, confidently claiming the two-hole spot in the batting order. Each swing I took was a blend of athleticism and power that Mr. Davis had taught me to be. Depending on the game situation, I chose finesse-putting balls in play with authority, carefully swatting singles. Other times, I unleashed raw power, driving the ball into the gaps of the outfield.

As a center fielder, my reflexes had to be lightning-fast, a feat achieved through countless hours of grueling training. Anticipating the ball's trajectory and making split-second decisions was an integral part of my role, and I reveled in it.

Transitioning to the NCAA D1 level of college baseball was a challenge, the increased pace of the game was a reality check. I had to adjust my timing at the plate, my stance, and my expectations to compete against the best future professional players in the prestigious PAC-10 conference.

Off the field, I was a history major at the University of Southern California. My passion for history was rooted in my desire to traverse the world and explore the past of my Italian ancestors. Balancing academics and sports were a tough task, but with discipline and a carefully planned routine, I managed.

Being a two-time NCAA D1 All-American Centerfielder and a regular in the prestigious Cape Cod summer league, I was already on the radar of Major League Baseball scouts. Their interest in me was a nod to my potential, fueling my drive to strive for more.

In all, I wasn't just playing a game. With each swing, each catch, each sprint, I was moving closer to my dream. Every time I stepped onto the field; I was doing more than just playing - I was letting my dreams take flight.

My college years seemed to fly by. I earned all-conference and all-American honors during my sophomore and junior seasons. I also won several Player of the Week and Month accolades in recognition of my performances during the season.

Sometimes I think about what would have happened if I had allowed myself to go to those parties everyone talked about. I never was much of a social person, but I may have met somebody or known what a broken heart felt like by then. But I felt confident with the decisions I had made. And if I had the chance to relive my college days, I wouldn't have it any other way.

As my junior year in college drew to a close, I faced the most crucial decision of my life: whether to pursue a career in professional baseball or stay in school and complete my senior year. Being a major league player had always been my dream, and with the upcoming MLB draft, I knew I would have a chance at being selected.

The lure of the major leagues had a gravitational pull that tugged at my heartstrings and whispered promises of fulfillment and achievement. It was an opportunity that would allow me to live out my childhood dreams and leave an indelible mark on the world of baseball. I decided to seize the opportunity that lay before me. I was prepared to take that leap of faith and dive headfirst into professional sports. The decision was not borne out of a desire for instant gratification or the allure of fame but rather a deep-seated understanding that this was my destiny — a path that had been paved by my sweat, tears, and unyielding determination that had carried me thus far.

As I prepared to embark on this new chapter of my life, I was acutely aware of the challenges that awaited me. The road to the major leagues was filled with physical and mental obstacles. But I was undeterred because I had been shaped and molded by setbacks for this very moment. As I was leaving college baseball, I knew that the world of minor-league baseball would determine my ultimate goal of becoming a major-league baseball player.

Stepping onto New Grounds

The MLB draft's buzz, unfolding in my very own hometown of Willow Creek, was palpable. My old school friends, previous teachers, notable townsfolk, and my three stalwart cheerleaders—Mr. Davis and my parents—filled the local community center. My heart pounded in anticipation as I'd been tipped off by scouts and several MLB executives that I'd likely be one of the first 75 players chosen. The decisive moment arrived as the San Francisco Giants announced their pick. With each word, the crowd erupted in cheers. "With the 33rd selection in the 1984 Major League Draft, the San Francisco Giants select Jack Thompson, Centerfielder, University of Southern California." Goosebumps spread across my skin as I absorbed the weight of those words—I was officially an MLB draftee. Willow Creek erupted with pride, celebrating alongside me. It was a testament to the countless hours of training, the sacrifices, and the unwavering belief in my abilities." The usually subdued Willow Creek erupted with pride. Images of me, from my youthful days in the local little league to my high school glory days, began appearing everywhere, cementing my hometown hero status.

My parents, who migrated from Italy to America in 1963, were brimming with joy, pride, and relief. They had watched me tirelessly train and persevere. Mr. Davis, my mentor, and a former MLB star shortstop was unable to hide his tearful happiness. He had guided me into becoming a top-tier outfielder, imparting invaluable tips and wisdom. In me, he saw his legacy and a heart-wrenching reminder of the son he lost in Vietnam. He was elated to witness me continue the journey upon which he had embarked.

My shift to the San Francisco Giants minor league system would be a steep learning curve. Despite being a high draft pick, I would be just another minor league hopeful among many, and I had to prove my worth all over again.

On the day I got drafted by the San Francisco Giants, a stark reality struck me. Professional baseball was no longer an aspiration but my current reality and, I hoped, my future. I was swapping the sun-drenched stadiums of Southern California for the grueling reality of minor-league baseball.

I still remember the day I signed my minor league contract. As I signed my name, a whirlpool of emotions took over. From being the awkward kid on the sandlot to becoming an All-American Centerfielder at USC, my journey had been nothing short of miraculous. It felt surreal, filled with pride, gratitude, and an inexplicable sense of calmness, as if my destiny had finally intertwined with my dreams. But I knew the road ahead was still littered with challenges. As always, I was prepared to face them head-on. But now, as I stepped onto the grounds of the spring training home of the Giants, in Scottsdale, Arizona, reality sank in. I was no longer just dreaming of playing professional baseball; it was my current reality. The sun-drenched stadiums of Southern California had given way to the grueling challenges of the minor leagues. This was where dreams were forged, where talents were tested, and where I had to prove my worth once again.

Minor-league baseball was an initiation by fire. Every player I came across was a potential major leaguer, each game was a test of my skills, character, and grit. Adjusting to new cities, teams, and routines was essential. Each day was unique, but my dedication to baseball was unwavering.

The first day I set foot in the locker room is etched in my memory. Other gifted players surrounded me, each with their dreams and narratives. The atmosphere was heavy with anticipation, determination, and the unmistakable scent of new leather. We were all puzzle pieces, each striving to make our mark and claim our place in professional baseball. The minor leagues proved to be a transient world, with players coming and going, constantly moving through the ranks and onto different rosters. It was a whirlwind of faces, names, and stories passing by, but amid this impermanence, I found solace and strength in the friendships I forged.

One of the first teammates I connected with was Miguel Dominguez, an outgoing and energetic infielder from the Dominican Republic. From the moment we met, his infectious spirit and love for the game were evident. Miguel had a charisma that drew people in, and his passion for baseball was unmatched. We bonded over our shared dreams of making it to the major leagues, swapping stories of our childhood sandlot games and the challenges we faced to get to where we were.

Miguel brought a certain joy and lightness to the team, always reminding us to have fun and enjoy the journey. Whether it was his contagious laughter in the dugout or his celebratory dance moves after a big win, he had a way of lifting everyone's spirits. Despite the language barrier, we communicated through our shared love for the game, and that was enough to form a deep bond.

Another teammate who became an integral part of our trio was Tyler Berry, a quiet but fiercely dedicated pitcher from the small town of Gonzales located in Texas. Tyler had been drafted straight out of high school, and his work ethic was unparalleled. He was the kind of guy who stayed late after practice, honing his craft, and constantly striving to improve. His determination inspired us all and pushed us to give our best.

While Tyler may not have been the most vocal on the team, his actions spoke volumes. He was a man of faith and always there to offer support, lending a listening ear or providing a reassuring pat on the back when things got tough. His calm and composed demeanor had a grounding effect on our group, reminding us to stay focused and composed amidst the chaos of the minor leagues.

Together, the three of us formed an enduring brotherhood. We shared the difficulties of our journey, celebrating the victories and comforting each other through the defeats. We became each other's support system, offering words of encouragement and motivation when doubts crept in. We were not just teammates; we were friends who understood the struggles and sacrifices that came with pursuing our dreams.

Amid the demanding schedule, the long bus rides, and the grueling workouts, Miguel, Tyler, and I found solace in each other's company. We spent countless hours discussing strategy, analyzing games, and sharing our hopes and fears. We pushed each other to be better, holding each other accountable and constantly striving to raise the bar.

Outside of the baseball field, we explored the new cities we found ourselves in, immersing ourselves in the local culture and savoring the small moments of joy that came with being on the road. We would go out for meals together, seeking out the best local spots for a taste of home or a new culinary adventure. These shared experiences forged a bond that extended beyond the confines of the game.

Through it all, Miguel, Tyler, and I remained united in our pursuit of our ultimate goal—reaching the major leagues. We knew that the road would be challenging and uncertain but having each other by our sides gave us strength and resilience. We lifted each other up when we stumbled, offered words of wisdom when doubts arose, and celebrated every milestone and accomplishment as a team.

As we faced the trials and tribulations of the minor leagues together, we grew not only as players but as individuals. We learned the value of perseverance, resilience, and the unwavering belief in ourselves and each other. Our friendship became an anchor in the ever-changing world of the minor leagues, grounding us and reminding us of the bigger picture.

And as we stepped onto the field each day, ready to give it our all, we knew that we were not alone. We had each other's backs, ready to support and uplift one another through the highs and lows. Our friendship became a source of strength, a reminder that we were in this together, and that no matter where our paths may lead, the bonds we formed in the minor leagues would endure.

My first assignment was in Scottsdale Arizona for the rookie league. The extreme heat, harsh fields, and almost empty stands were a stark contrast to USC's adoring crowds and lush fields. This, however, was the starting line of my professional journey.

Being a minor leaguer was markedly different from my college days. My daily routine no longer revolved around classes, study sessions, and college games. Instead, it consisted of early morning workouts, long bus rides, and endless baseball games. This was baseball in its purest form, devoid of the glamor and fame of the major leagues. The accommodations were modest, the pay was minimal, and the road trips were exhausting. It was a stark reminder that I had to earn my place in the professional ranks.

I quickly learned that talent alone would not be enough to navigate the minor leagues. It required mental fortitude, resilience, and an unwavering belief in myself. Every player in the minors was chasing the same dream, and the competition was fierce. Each at-bat, each fielding opportunity was a chance to prove myself to the coaches, scouts, and the organization.

As I embarked on this challenging journey, I found solace in the familiar rhythms of the game. The crack of the bat, the thud of the ball hitting the glove, and the synchronized movements of a well-executed double play grounded me amidst the whirlwind of my new life.

My first season in the minors was a humbling experience. I quickly realized that I wasn't the star player I had been in college. The pitchers threw harder, the fielders were more skilled, and the game demanded more from me at every turn. I faced setbacks and struggled to find my footing. But I refused to let those challenges define me. Instead, I saw them as opportunities for growth.

Every failure became a lesson, a chance to learn, improve, and refine my skills. And every small triumph, no matter how insignificant it seemed, felt like a monumental victory. As the season progressed, I gradually adjusted to the pace and intensity of professional baseball. I began to find my rhythm and regain my confidence.

But there were moments of doubt, moments when I questioned myself and my abilities. In those moments, I would recall the wisdom imparted by Mr. Davis during our countless conversations on the sandlot and throughout my college career. He had once told me, "The game of baseball is a lot like life, Jack. It's about adapting, taking the hits, and always moving forward." Those words echoed in my mind, reminding me to stay resilient and keep pushing through adversity.

As our first minor league season ended, Tyler and I agreed that we would try to be minor league roommates at next season's spring training. I felt that I could keep a watch over Tyler and help him as a mentor much like Mr. Davis had been to me over the years. We shook hands as the airport van pulled up to our minor league complex to take me to the airport for my flight home to Willow Creek. I was looking forward to catching my breath and returning to my hometown for some rest as well as recharging my inner batteries to prepare for my first full season as a minor leaguer.

That fall, after completing my first season in the minor leagues, I finally returned home to Willow Creek. It had been a while since I had set foot in my hometown, and as I walked its familiar streets, I realized how much it had changed. What was once a small and ordinary place had transformed into a comforting refuge from the pressures of professional baseball. It was a reminder of where I came from, a grounding force that kept me connected to my roots.

During the offseason, while the world around me was quiet, I poured my heart and soul into training. I knew that if I wanted to come back stronger for the next season, I had to push myself harder than ever before. Every morning, I would wake up early, hit the gym, and practice relentlessly. I honed my skills, fine-tuned my technique, and worked on improving every aspect of my game. There were no shortcuts, no easy paths to success. I knew that the road ahead would be challenging, but I was determined to embrace it.

During my training, I made it a point to visit Mr. Davis as often as I could. He was not only my mentor but also a dear friend who had played a significant role in shaping my journey. I secretly hoped that spending time with him would unlock the great mystery of how to become a major leaguer. We would sit together, sharing stories and laughter, as I eagerly asked him questions. And every time, his response would be the same, filled with wisdom and simplicity: "The game is the same, Jack, as it always has been. The secret is to have fun and let your mind work for you, not against you!"

Those words resonate deeply within me. They reminded me of the joy I had felt as a child playing the game, the pure love for baseball that had ignited my passion. It was a powerful reminder that amidst the pressures and expectations of the professional world, I needed to find that childlike joy again. Mr. Davis's guidance was a guiding light, reminding me that success wasn't just about physical skills but also about the mental aspect of the game.

Looking back, I wished I could have taken Mr. Davis with me on those long bus rides throughout the minor leagues. Those journeys were often arduous, filled with fatigue and uncertainty. Having him by my side would have been a source of comfort and inspiration, a guiding presence to keep my mind in a good place. But even though he couldn't physically be there, his words and teachings remained with me, guiding me through the highs and lows.

As the offseason came to an end, I felt a renewed sense of purpose and determination. Spring training awaited, along with my first full season of minor league baseball. The road ahead was still uncertain, filled with challenges and obstacles. But armed with the lessons I had learned and the unwavering support of my family and mentors like Mr. Davis, I was ready to face whatever lay ahead.

The journey was far from over. The dream of stepping onto a major league field still burned brightly within me. But as I prepared to embark on my second season, I knew that the foundation had been set. I understood the importance of my roots, the power of embracing the game with joy, and the value of having mentors who believed in me. Willow Creek would always be my home, the place that grounded me and reminded me of who I was.

With a grateful heart, I took a final look at my hometown, knowing that it had shaped me into the person and player I had become. As I stepped onto the path that led me back to the world of baseball, I carried with me the lessons, memories, and friendships that had been forged in the minor leagues. The journey continued, and I was ready!

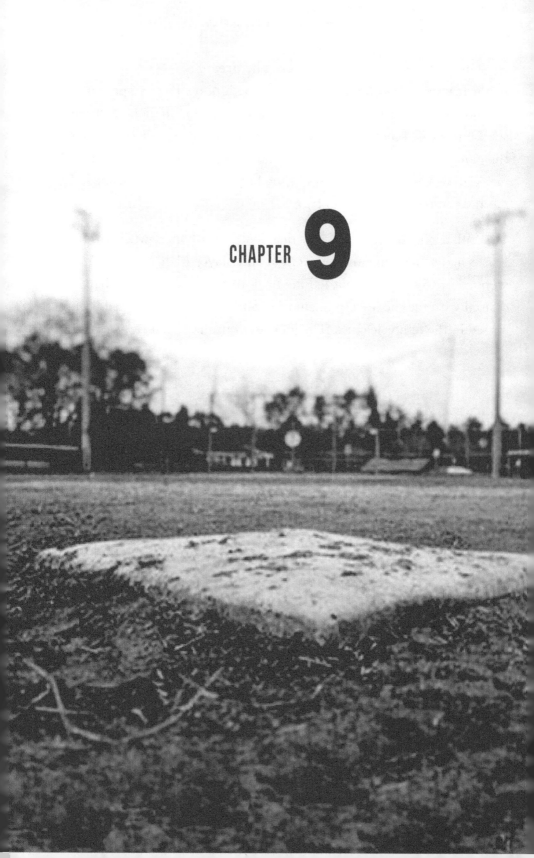

The Journey to the Majors

Spring training in Scottsdale, Arizona, began a new chapter in our baseball journey. The sun beat down on the field as Miguel, Tyler, and I gathered, filled with excitement and nerves. This was our chance to prove ourselves, display our skills, and take one step closer to our dreams of reaching the Major Leagues.

As the days turned into weeks, we immersed ourselves in the rigorous training regimen. The early morning workouts, grueling practices, games, and intense drills pushed us to our limits. We faced triumphs and setbacks during those long days but always kept sight of our goal.

Amidst the sweat and fatigue, our conversations were filled with cautious optimism. We discussed the upcoming season, wondering what team we would be assigned to after spring training. The competition was fierce, with talented players vying for limited spots. But we remained focused, supporting each other and believing in our abilities.

Finally, the day came when the rosters were announced. I felt excited and relieved as I learned I had made the High-A San Jose team. Miguel and Tyler were assigned to low A Augusta. This was a moment for the three of us to understand that while baseball is a great game, it is a tough business, they were headed east, and I was headed north, as in Northern California. This was a significant step forward, and I couldn't help but think of the journey that had brought me to this point.

Playing close to my hometown filled me with pride and determination. The thought of having my family, friends, and Mr. Davis, my lifelong mentor, watching me play in person for the first time as a professional athlete gave me an extra boost of motivation. I wanted to make them proud and show them that their support had not been in vain.

The season kicked off with a mix of nerves and excitement. The stands were filled with eager fans, their cheers echoing through the ballpark. I felt the weight of the game on my shoulders, but I knew I had prepared for this moment. I stepped onto the field, ready to give it my all.

As the season progressed, the pressure mounted, and every game felt like a critical opportunity to prove myself. The days became a blur of practices, games, and relentless self-evaluation. I worked tirelessly to improve my skills, seeking guidance from coaches, studying game footage, and fine-tuning every aspect of my game.

One summer evening, the San Jose Giants were facing off against the Modesto Nuts in what turned out to be a fiercely contested game. The sun began to dip below the horizon, casting a warm, golden glow over the field. The stands were filled with fans, their cheers and applause creating an electric atmosphere.

I stood in the on-deck circle, my heart pounding in anticipation as I prepared to step up to the plate. My mind was focused, my eyes locked on the pitcher. A familiar figure caught my eye just as I was about to step into the batter's box. There, standing by the railing near the dugout, was George Davis himself. My heart skipped a beat as I locked eyes with him. It felt like a mirage, a figment of my imagination, but the smile on his weathered face reassured me that he was really there. At that moment, I felt like I was back at the sandlot in Willow Creek; the game was the same, just at a different level.

With newfound determination, I stepped into the batter's box. My lifelong mentor, George Davis, was in the stands watching me play as a professional athlete for the first time. The weight of his presence and the memories of our time together flooded my mind.

The pitcher wound up and delivered the first pitch. It came in fast, but I stayed focused, precisely tracking the ball's trajectory. With a swift swing of the bat, I made solid contact, sending the ball soaring toward the outfield. The crowd held its breath as the ball sailed higher and higher, clearing the outfield fence with room to spare.

A rush of exhilaration coursed through me as I rounded the bases, my eyes momentarily meeting George's. He tipped his hat with a nod, a silent gesture of pride and approval. At that moment, I knew he had seen my potential long before I had seen it in myself.

The game continued, and I felt an extra surge of confidence with George's presence in the stands. I made diving catches in the outfield, stole bases with daring speed, and delivered key hits to drive in runs. Each play was a tribute to the man who had taught me to love this game.

After the game, I rushed to the dugout to find George waiting for me. His eyes gleamed with emotion as he enveloped me in a bear hug. "You did it, Jack," he said, his voice choked with pride. "You've come a long way, and you're just getting started. Always remember the game is always the same; allow yourself to let the little boy in you have fun!"

Tears welled in my eyes as I clung to George, my voice trembling with gratitude. "Thank you, Mr. Davis. Your belief in me has been my driving force all these years."

He smiled warmly, placing a hand on my shoulder. "You were always meant for greatness, Jack. I saw it in you from the very beginning. Keep pushing, growing, and never forget where you came from."

Standing there with George, I realized this surprise visit was more meaningful than I could have imagined. It was a reminder of the journey we had taken together, the sandlots we had played on, and the dreams we had nurtured.

From that day on, I carried George's presence with me, not just in my heart but also on the field. Whenever doubt crept in or the pressure mounted, I would glance up to the stands, imagining him there, tipping his hat, and cheering me on.

The season continued, and my performance drew the attention of the Giants' roving instructors. Word of my progress reached the higher-ups, and in late May, the news I had been waiting for arrived. I was getting called up to Double-A in Richmond, Virginia.

As I packed my bags for the next chapter of my journey, I couldn't help but think of George Davis's impact on my life. His surprise visit to the San Jose game would forever be etched as a turning point in my career.

The journey was far from over, but with George's wisdom in my heart and the Sandlot Legacy as my guiding light, I stepped onto the next stage of my baseball odyssey, eager to embrace the challenges and triumphs that awaited me.

The Giant's roving instructors observed my progress from a distance throughout the season. The Giants had a reputation as elite talent evaluators and trusted their top prospects with these instructors. The focus on developing top prospects instilled both fear and respect in me. I knew that earning their approval would require not just skill but mental fortitude as well.

In late May, the news I had been waiting for arrived. I was called up to Double-A in Richmond, Virginia. It was a promotion that brought a mix of elation and anxiety. I knew this was a significant step closer to the Majors, but I also understood that the challenges would be more critical.

My first weeks in Double-A were a test of resilience. I faced tougher pitchers, faster baserunners, and more experienced fielders. The game seemed to move at lightning speed, and I had to adjust quickly. There were moments when I struggled with mistakes that I had never made before.

As the summer wore on, I worked tirelessly to improve my game. Rusty's presence loomed over me, a constant reminder of the expectations I had to meet. His coaching style was challenging and demanding, pushing me to my limits. There were moments when I questioned whether I could live up to his standards.

One game stands out in my memory. It was a tight contest, with the bases loaded and two outs in the late innings. I stepped up to the plate, feeling the weight of the moment. But instead of rising to the occasion, I let my frustration get the best of me. I swung wildly at a pitch, missing it completely, and I knew I had let my team down.

In that moment of defeat, Rusty's voice cut through the silence. "Thompson! Pick up your helmet!" he yelled. His words were stern and commanding, leaving no room for argument. I felt embarrassed and ashamed as I retrieved my helmet, realizing the lesson he was trying to teach me.

After the game, Rusty took me aside. He looked me in the eyes, his gaze unwavering. "Jack, you have the talent but need to trust yourself," he said. "Baseball is a game of failure, and how you respond to that failure defines you. You must embrace the moment, stay present, and compete with all you have. Let the results come naturally."

His words struck a chord deep within me. I realized that I had been putting too much pressure on myself, allowing the weight of expectations to overwhelm me. I needed to find joy in the game again, trust my abilities, and let go of the fear of failure.

From that day forward, I approached each game with a newfound freedom. I focused on the process, giving my best effort and letting the results care for themselves. I embraced the highs and the lows, understanding that each setback was an opportunity for growth.

The season progressed, and with each passing game, I grew more confident and resilient. The setbacks became fewer, and the successes more frequent. I knew I was inching closer to my dream, to the elusive call to the Majors.

One summer evening, as the setting sunbathed the field in a warm, golden glow, I stood in the outfield of a Double-A stadium. The crowd's roar was louder than in the lower minors. The energy was electric, a palpable reminder that the major leagues were just a few steps away. Despite the pressure, I felt strangely at peace, like I always did on a baseball field. I belonged here, and I was ready to take that ultimate step.

As the game progressed, I found myself in the batter's box, the weight of the bat familiar and comforting in my hands. The pitcher, a seasoned veteran, stared me down from the mound. He wound up, and the pitch came hurtling toward me. I swung, and there was that familiar crack of the bat, the exhilarating sensation of perfect contact. The ball soared high into the air, arcing towards the outfield.

I ran, my heart pounding in my chest. Rounding first, I stole a glance toward the outfield. The fielder was racing toward the ball, but it was too late. The ball cleared the fence with room to spare. A home run. The roar of the crowd was deafening as I trotted around the bases. The feeling was indescribable. It wasn't just the joy of hitting a home run but the realization that I was ready. I was prepared for the major leagues.

The sun was beginning to set, casting a golden glow over the baseball field as I walked off the diamond toward our dugout, feeling exhaustion and contentment. The game had been a hard-fought battle, and I had given it my all, as I always did. I noticed a figure waiting for me near the dugout as I approached the clubhouse. It was Rusty, with whom I had built a strong bond throughout the season.

Rusty had been a fixture in the minor leagues for two decades, dedicating his life to the game and the development of young players like me. With a grizzled face that bore the weight of experience and a twinkle in his eye, Rusty had become a trusted mentor and friend to many aspiring ballplayers.

As I approached Rusty, I noticed a mix of excitement and something else—a hint of bittersweet emotion—in his eyes. He cleared his throat, a subtle sign of nervousness, before finally finding his voice.

"Jack, can we have a moment?" Rusty asked, his tone a blend of solemnity and anticipation.

Curiosity and a flutter of nerves swirled within me as I nodded and followed Rusty to a quiet corner of the dugout. The atmosphere felt heavy with anticipation, and my heart pounded as I braced for whatever news awaited me.

Rusty looked directly into my eyes, his gaze filled with pride and sadness. "Kid, I've got some news for you," he began, his voice trembling with a combination of emotions. "You've been called up. I spoke with the GM, and they need you in San Fran."

My heart skipped a beat, a whirlwind of emotions crashing over me like a tidal wave. The words hung in the air, and I struggled to comprehend their significance. The magnitude of the moment weighed heavily on my shoulders as if the dreams I had nurtured since childhood were suddenly becoming a tangible reality.

Tears welled in my eyes as I looked at Rusty, my voice choked with gratitude. "Thank you, Rusty. Thank you for everything. I couldn't have reached this moment without your guidance and belief in me."

Rusty placed a weathered hand on my shoulder, his voice filled with pride and genuine affection. "You've earned this, kid. Every swing, sprint, and bit of heart you've poured into this game has led you to this moment. The road ahead won't be easy, but I know you have what it takes. Remember where you came from; remember the love for the game that brought you here. Embrace this opportunity and play with all the fire and passion that's carried you this far."

I nodded, my emotions threatening to overwhelm me. I knew that Rusty's words held a lifetime of wisdom, a reminder to honor the journey that had brought me to this point. It was a realization that the sandlot dreams of my youth were now merging with the grand stage of the major leagues.

In that dugout, under the fading rays of the setting sun, Rusty and I shared a moment of profound connection. Our shared love for the game and the transformative power it held were encapsulated in our unspoken understanding. It was the passing of the torch, a recognition that I was ready to take the next step, to embrace the challenges and triumphs that awaited me.

As I walked away, my heart bursting with a renewed sense of purpose, I knew Rusty's words would be etched into my very being. I was prepared to carry the lessons, the passion, and the spirit of the sandlot with me as I stepped onto the grand stage of the major leagues. And as I picked up my phone to make the most important calls of my life—to Mr. Davis and my parents—I couldn't help but feel a sense of awe at the incredible journey that had brought me to this extraordinary moment.

With trembling hands, I reached for my phone and dialed Mr. Davis's number. He had been my mentor and guiding light throughout my baseball journey, always offering wisdom and encouragement. The phone rang, and my heart raced in anticipation. Finally, Mr. Davis's voice came through the line, filled with warmth and familiarity.

"Hello?" Mr. Davis answered, his voice tinged with curiosity.

"Hey, Mr. Davis, it's Jack," I said, my voice filled with excitement and nervousness. "I have some incredible news."

Mr. Davis paused for a moment, sensing the anticipation in my voice. "Well, don't keep me waiting, young man. What's this incredible news?"

"I'm getting called up to the major leagues, Mr. Davis!" I exclaimed, my voice cracking with emotion. "All those years of hard work and dedication have paid off. I'm going to be playing in the big leagues."

There was a long pause and a gut-wrenching silence on the other end of the line. I could hear sniffling, he took a deep breath, and then Mr. Davis's voice trembled with pride and joy. "Jack, my boy, I can't express how proud I am of you. This is a moment you've been working towards your whole life. Remember, stay focused, stay humble, and give it your all. The sandlot kid from Willow Creek will shine on the grandest stage."

Tears welled in my eyes as I absorbed Mr. Davis's words of wisdom. "Thank you, Mr. Davis. Your guidance and support have meant the world to me. I couldn't have done it without you. You have always been like a father to me, and I promise to make you proud!" me,

After saying our goodbyes, I took a deep breath and dialed my parents' number. My heart pounded as the phone rang, and I imagined the surprise and joy that would spread across their faces when I shared the news.

"Hello?" my mother's voice came through the line, filled with warmth and love.

"Hey, Mom, it's Jack," I said, my voice filled with excitement.

"Jack, sweetheart, is everything okay?" my mother asked, concerned about lacing her words.

"More than okay, Mom," I replied, my voice quivering with emotion. "I just got the call. I'm getting called up to the major leagues. Can you believe it?"

My mother's gasp was audible through the phone, followed by stunned silence. And then, she erupted into a chorus of joyful tears and laughter. "Oh, my baby! I knew this day would come. Your father and I are so proud of you. We always knew you had it in you."

Tears streamed down my face as I listened to my mother's words of love and support. My father's voice joined in, a mix of pride and excitement, as we celebrated the incredible news together. It was a moment of pure bliss, a culmination of years of sacrifice and dedication.

As I hung up the phone, I sat in the quiet clubhouse, overcome with many emotions. The sandlot, Mr. Davis, and my parents had all played an integral role in my journey. They believed in me when I doubted myself, pushing me to become the best version of myself.

After years of arduous work, sweat, and countless sacrifices, my dream would become a reality. I was going to be a major league baseball player. As I packed my bags for San Francisco, I thought about the long journey that had led me to this point. From the sandlot games of my youth, through the triumphs and heartbreaks of high school and college, to the grueling grind of the minor leagues, every step has shaped me and prepared me for this moment.

As the plane took off, heading towards my new future, I stared out the window, my heart filled with anticipation. The dream that had started on a makeshift sandlot in Willow Creek was about to come true. But more than that, I knew that this was just the beginning. The journey was far from over; it was only just starting. The major leagues awaited, and I was ready to face whatever challenges they would bring.

CHAPTER 10

The Rookie Season

My first season in the major leagues was a whirlwind of new experiences, challenges, defeats, and victories as I played alongside some of the world's most talented athletes, each with unique stories and varied journeys to the big leagues. The level of play was more intense than anything I had ever experienced. Still, I was determined to prove that I belonged nowhere but among the best. I would rise to the challenge.

In the beginning, I had to face my share of struggles as I adjusted to the speed and skill of the Major League game. The pitchers were more cunning, the hitters more powerful, and the stakes higher. Every time I doubted myself, I looked back to that summer in the sandlot and saw the kid I was walking with into the field, thinking about what he would say on those summer days if someone had told him how far we would make it.

The kid who loved baseball above everything else was still alive inside me. With every pitch, with every at-bat, with the sound of every cheer, I could feel him crying out with happiness. The nerves were always there; that feeling that this was a dream would never leave me. But it was so real. So real that I was still trying to believe it.

As the season progressed, I began to find my footing in the major leagues earning the respect of my teammates and coaches. I continued pushing myself, constantly seeking to improve and learn from the professionals surrounding me. It was part of my DNA. I didn't care if I had to work ten times harder than anybody else; I belonged there. I owed it to the kid I was.

I experienced many triumphs with my team, filled with teammates who were great professionals. The stands went wild every time we played at home, chanting, and cheering us on. The feeling of being supported by so many people was powerful, immeasurable. From center field, I felt so small and yet so big that I couldn't help but wonder if it was all just magic.

The magic of baseball.

Every victory was a conquest. Our fans greeted us at each game with words of admiration and affection that could make anyone feel like more than just a baseball player. Of course, when there was defeat, some words of encouragement and appreciation morphed into scorn and disdain. It didn't matter that we had given it our all on the field; some of the fans would get so angry with us that they seemed capable of doing something crazy.

It was easy to disengage from this world and sometimes necessary to disconnect to stay sane. The fans could easily take you to heaven or drag you twenty feet underground. Luckily, every time that happened, Mr. Davis's words came back to my mind, reminding me that the most critical thing was seeking balance in my life and finding people who would help me stay grounded and authentic.

This was no more evident in my career than in my first game. My family and closest friends had managed to be there that day, cheering me on from the stands. I could feel their presence in my bones. That was the first time I felt unstoppable... invincible. Being there, fulfilling my life's dream, and knowing that the people I loved most were there to see me is something I will never be able to put into words.

I tried not to glance up at where my parents were seated. If I looked in their direction, I would have been overcome with emotion. My parents had given everything for me, working more hours than what was required of any loving parent. But they did it dutifully to provide me with the best. Their goal was to ensure that I only had to worry about being a kid and playing baseball. Although they hadn't been able to be by my side for most of my life, I knew that my triumphs had been thanks to them.

That first game will always remain vivid in my memory. After batting, my heart stopped momentarily when I realized my nerves hadn't gotten the best of me, and I had hit the ball exactly how I wanted to. I ran as fast as I could until I rounded first base. Still, I could feel my heart pounding. As I stood on first base, looking at my third base coach, my body and mind were divided instantly between whether I would choose to steal second base as I had been given the green light. If I were able to get a good jump, I could take it.

The count was even at one ball and one strike, and I thought the next pitch would be a breaking ball, allowing me an opportunity to steal second base. I guessed right and got a good jump after the breaking ball hit the dirt. I easily beat the throw and was safe at second base. The crowd erupted as I dusted myself off, standing alone at second base. I will never forget how the world vanished around me, and the only thing left was baseball.

That first game would go down in my memory as proof that I had made it — an official major league regular. My dream and everything

I had worked so hard for since little league and my days on the sandlot were meaningful to those who had been by my side from the beginning. Those who were there even when my dream seemed impossible and believed in me. They were the co-architects of my success. They believed in me even when there was no reason to do so. They had faith in me when I didn't. They were always there; whether I failed or succeeded, they would always be with me.

All those hours of impossible workouts, the fatigue, the burning in my muscles, the air not reaching my lungs... all that made me a better player. But it wouldn't make me who I was that day. That day I repaid my parents, my friends, and Mr. Davis for all the leaps of faith they had taken on my behalf by showing the world that Jack Thompson, a simple kid from Willow Creek, deserved to be where he was — and he was here to stay.

God, it felt so good.

But not all was fun and glorious in my rookie season. If my first game was unforgettable, the first loss taught me what a broken heart felt like. The truth is, I don't know exactly what went wrong that afternoon when I lost my first game. But I know the opposing team did a better job than we did.

As that game went on, my heart was deflating. The stands kept cheering us on, reminding us that we still had a chance to win. But it didn't seem to be our day. We made a few errors, and our bats, that on previous occasions had been red hot, suddenly went ice cold. The few baserunners we did have never got past second base the entire game. Do you know the feeling when everything that can go wrong will go wrong? Like Murphy's law but on an awful day in the middle of a baseball game.

As the game entered the later innings, we all felt devastated that we were too far behind to pull out a win. And we began to feel even worse when the same crowd realized it, too, and began to boo us for losing to what they considered an inferior team from across the bay. It's impossible to explain the immense disappointment rushing at me that afternoon. It started my first extended slump at the big-league level. I felt as if everything I had gone through and all the effort I had invested had suddenly disappeared to expose that kid who was always picked last in every game. I felt smaller than I had ever felt before, and for a moment, I just wanted to hide. For a moment, I just wanted to throw myself on my bed and cry out of powerlessness. I worried that I might even be sent down to the minor leagues.

One night, all I wanted to do was to try and sleep, especially after the scolding we got from the manager for being easily distracted and failing at the simplest things. We explained our failure as a difficult day, an awful day. But that needed to be better when you played at the level we were at, the big leagues. The next day I called my dad, partly to be cheered up and partly to warn him that my great major league career might be ending.

"Hey, Dad. How are you? How's Mom?"

"Hello, son. We're fine, thank you. Your mom is in the kitchen, preparing lunch. We're having a picnic today."

Since they retired, they had started making plans every day. My parents were trying to make up for the time lost between them because of years and years of work raising their family. I admired them for it. I even wished that, at some point, I would find someone to share the love I had seen between them. "And you, how are you today, Jack? Rough game yesterday, kiddo?"

"Oh, no, please, Dad. Tell me you didn't see yesterday's game." I remember the embarrassment spread all over my body, accompanied by the fear of being a disappointment. It was as if, after that disastrous game, the insecure child had returned to make me doubt my ability again.

"Of course, I saw it, Jack. I see all your games, son. Yesterday was a terrific one, don't you think?"

I still don't know if it was seconds, minutes, or hours. But hearing my father laugh at the disaster of the previous day's game robbed me of the ability to speak. All those insecurities I had buried so deep inside me were coming to the surface by the minute. I felt like success was slipping away and worried I would never pick up a bat at the big league again. Suddenly, everything I had fought for threatened to go down the drain.

"Are you still there, buddy?" he said.

I didn't realize how long I had sat silently, stewing in my pain and grief. I must have made a sound, so he knew I was still listening. But I don't remember.

"Jack, listen to me. It was just one game, not the end of the world. The season's long; focus on the next one, and you will be fine. You didn't think you would win 150 games, right? Losing a game doesn't make you less of a player; it makes you better. Remember when it was all about having fun in the sandlot? This is the same but with crazy crowds included."

"No, Dad. This is the Major Leagues! This is not about having fun; this is about—"

"Remember that talk you told me about with Mr. Davis, Jack? You asked me about the one later because you wanted to know if you understood it right."

"Which one, Dad? Mr. Davis could be very cryptic sometimes."

"The one about the car and the journey."

I did remember that talk. I nodded silently just as I realized we were on the phone, and he couldn't see me. That just made me feel even more stupid. Just one more blunder to add to the weight of the loss.

"I'll take that as a yes. You must remember that, as Mr. Davis said: Baseball is a vehicle that will lead you wherever you want. This last game is like having a flat tire on your car. Does it mean you won't make it to your destination? No, it means you must get out, change the tire, and keep driving! Enjoy the journey, son. Make as many stops as you need, meet people on the way, and remember, no matter how far you go, your family will always be here for you. And please, Jack, have fun. Remember, that's why you started in the first place. If you lose the fun of the game, you've lost everything."

Many things happened that year — victories and defeats. The former never stopped making me feel unstoppable, and the latter continued to break a little piece of my heart. But the words of Mr. Davis and my father were always with me, reminding me that sometimes the road wasn't straight but had bumps, difficulties, and unexpected stops designed to help me discover possibilities I didn't know existed.

As the season ended, I realized I had still managed to have fun and hadn't been sent down to the minors. Underneath all that pressure, the insecure kid had learned that having fun was a prerequisite for doing what you love most in the world. This was what Mr. Davis was referring to that summer, warning me to avoid the mindset where my life depended on the opinions of others. My view of myself and those close to me genuinely showed me who I was and what mattered most.

In time, I managed the losses as gracefully as the wins. I had learned more that summer than some people learned in a lifetime. Mr. Davis had prepared me for baseball, adulthood, fatherhood, and life. What he didn't tell me — what he never prepared me for — were those times when the people along for our life's journey were suddenly taken away.

That happened to me, and I was unprepared for the rush of pain that overtook me.

* * * * *

Mr. Davis's passing came unexpectedly. I was in the midst of a slump, struggling to maintain my starting outfield position with the San Francisco Giants. I was already feeling down, thinking I was about to be sent back down to the minors when I got hit with an even more significant blow. A call from Ben Driscoll, Mr. Davis's best friend, broke the news that George Davis had passed away peacefully in his sleep, a quiet end to a life filled with joy and sorrow.

My initial reaction was one of shock and disbelief. I felt a profound sense of loss as if a part of me had been taken away. It wasn't fair. I needed my mentor most during this time: his comfort, wisdom, and guidance. I remembered the countless hours we had spent together on the sandlot, the lessons I had learned, and the friendship we had forged.

The emotions came in waves. First shock, then denial, followed by anger and regret. With the busy life I had crafted as a major league player, I had not visited Mr. Davis as often as I used to before starting my career with the Giants.

As I boarded the plane to attend the funeral service, it took all my strength to hold back the tears and not break down. The funeral was a somber event, attended by many who had known and respected Mr. Davis. I had been asked to deliver the eulogy — an honor and a sobering obligation. I spoke of Mr. Davis's influence on my life, his teachings about baseball and life, and his enduring legacy. Others also shared stories, like Ben Driscoll, whose recounting of Mr. Davis's past gave me a deeper understanding of my mentor's life.

These stories painted a picture of a young George Davis, much like me, full of dreams and aspirations. Ben spoke of their friendly rivalry, shared dreams of playing on the All-Stars, and experiences as high school baseball team teammates. He also spoke of George's dedication and talent on the field, his inner conflicts and self-doubt, and his pursuit of his dream to become a professional baseball player.

I was overcome with emotion hearing Mr. Davis's struggles were very much like mine. He has battled the same self-doubt and pursued opportunities like mine. These stories resonated deeply with me. The parallels were uncanny. I was comforted that Mr. Davis struggled to balance his personal and professional lives, just like I was. He had successfully navigated the choppy waters of the major league, inspiring hope that I would too.

After the service, I stood by Mr. Davis's grave. The tombstone was a simple slab etched with the words "A beloved husband, father, and friend. A mentor on and off the field. His legacy lives on."

His legacy…

I was part of that legacy, as was every person whose life he touched. Standing before the grave, I felt a deep sense of regret and a renewed sense of purpose — a resolve to honor Mr. Davis's memory by living out the lessons he had taught him. This great man had made one thing clear: baseball was not just a game or a career but a journey, a series of thousands of moments to be experienced and appreciated.

I left the services determined to carry on Mr. Davis's legacy through several specific actions. First, I wrote Mr. Davis's name and uniform number under the brim of my baseball cap, a constant reminder of my mentor's presence and influence. I also wrote the words "BE PRESENT IN THE MIND AND BODY," the mantra that encapsulated Mr. Davis's teachings. Whenever I felt down or overwhelmed, I would take off my cap and read these words, drawing strength and inspiration from them.

The passing of Mr. Davis served as a pivotal moment in my life. It profoundly changed me, setting the stage for the rest of my journey. In truth, I felt a deep regret, a gnawing sense of missed opportunities. I had missed so much time with the man. And I wasn't there at the end to say goodbye. But there was also a blessing from returning to Willow Creek to mourn Mr. Davis's loss; the joy and passion I once felt for baseball, which had been overshadowed by the slump, was reignited. I had been lumbering under the weight of expectation and the fear of failure. But standing there beside Mr. Davis's grave, I could hear his voice:

"Baseball is as much a game of the mind as it is of the body, young man. Life and baseball are not about the destination; it's about enjoying the journey."

Once a source of inspiration, these words now felt like a brand-new challenge. A challenge to face my fears, confront my doubts, and find the strength to continue the journey Mr. Davis and I started together. Though there was a deep sadness, there was also a sense of resolve. I knew that Mr. Davis would not want me to give up. He would like me to fight, persevere, and find joy in the journey, no matter how difficult.

As I left the cemetery, I carried with me more than the weight of grief; I bore a renewed sense of purpose. I would honor Mr. Davis's memory, not by dwelling on his loss, but by living out the lessons he had taught me. I would face these new challenges head-on, preserving the joy in his journey and striving to be the best player and person I could be.

I stepped back onto the field, ready to end the slump. My family and friends, those who had been with me every step of the way, were there with me or watching television. But my heart kept returning to the missing person: Mr. Davis. It was a fight to not think every second about what he would have felt to see me standing in the middle of the field in the major leagues. How he would be happy to see me fulfill that dream that seemed so unattainable that first day he watched me play alone on the sandlot. Something inside me told me he was proud of me wherever he was.

There were moments when I thought I could hear him as clearly as if he were by my side: "Jack, my boy, move your feet. Be athletic. Look at the pitcher, his position. Don't lose sight of the ball. Before every pitch, be moving and stay loose. Breathe deep and follow your instincts."

He was a legend in my eyes.
And I… I was his legacy.

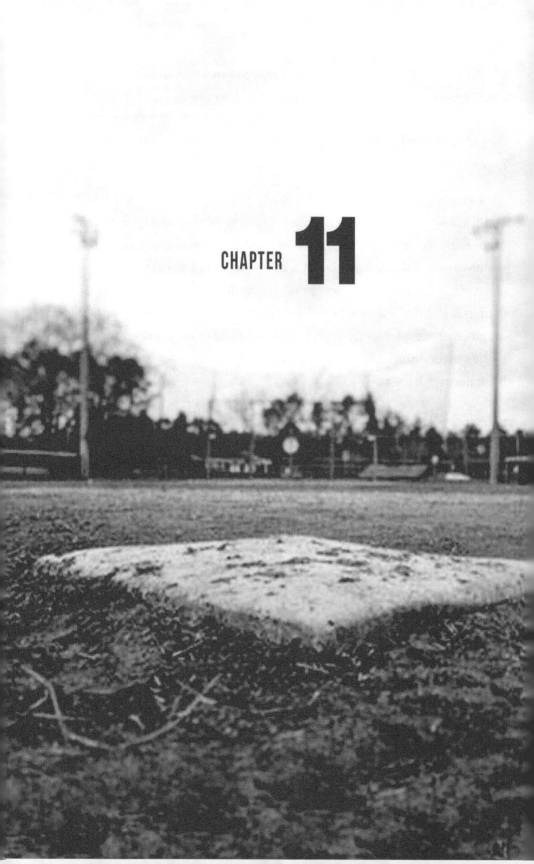

CHAPTER 11

All-Star Aspirations

As my career in the major leagues continued, I became a consistent and reliable player for my team. Over time, I developed a reputation for my hard work, dedication, and passion for the game. My determination caught the attention of fans and sports commentators alike. With that, something I'd never even dreamed of happened; I began to be mentioned as a potential candidate for the All-Star Game.

As a kid, I locked myself in my room and imagined what it would be like to walk onto the field of the major leagues, hearing the fans yell my name and feeling the surge of energy of my teammates beside me. The lights, the grass under my feet, the cameras, and the sound of baseballs hitting the bats. All of it. That was the greatest thing that could happen to someone like me. Once I got it, I thought I could never aspire higher, that I had reached my peak, and I just had to try to stay there as long as possible.

Now, looking back, I wonder what kind of a kid runs from his dreams because they are too far-fetched? When we used to play astronauts, it was as if someone would have told us, "Oh no, you can't play astronauts. Do you have a thousand hours of flight time or one of the master's degrees necessary to apply for the job? You don't? Well, put your feet on the ground then, guys."

It was just ridiculous. But that was me, a kid too aware of his insecurities to allow himself to dream aloud. Although, at that moment, without me needing to dream, an opportunity that had never crossed my mind began to grow inside me.

I had learned over the years that whether I won or lost, the important thing was to always remain humble and keep working hard every day. I didn't let my pride of grandeur swell my head and stayed close to the people who reminded me that everything would be fine despite my success. I was still just Jack Thompson, the Willow Creek Kid. And that's how I lived, trying to instill in children the value of effort and how it fosters the ability to overcome.

That's why I didn't know how to react when my teammates and coaches supported my candidacy for the All-Stars. It felt like the day I got that acceptance letter from Southern Cal. It wasn't something I had to work day and night to get, but it had fallen into my hands like a gift, and I wasn't used to it — or maybe I was incapable of getting used to things like that.

The thought of playing in the All-Star Game alongside the most talented players in the league was both exhilarating and intimidating. The honor would be a testament to my growth as a player and the countless hours of practice I had invested in fulfilling my dreams. However, the pressure to perform at such an important level started feeling overwhelming.

As always, I returned to Mr. Davis's words when I felt indecisive or unsure of my abilities. That old man had changed my life from beginning to end. He had given me a perspective I had never considered possible. He helped me become a man who puts the people he loves first and foremost. Before every game, I rehearsed his words: "Baseball is a game of the mind as it is for the body, kiddo." Those words kept me focused, grounded, and determined to give my best.

As he predicted, over the years, I came to understand his teachings better. I understood that grateful attitude for everything life put in his way, without believing himself more than just a human, without blabbing about everything he had lived through. Strangely, he didn't say who he was when we met. I remember thinking that if it had been me, I would have gone around Willow Creek with a sign proclaiming that a baseball star lived there. But now I know that whatever we do, we are just men playing the game we love and doing what makes us happy.

Happiness and sadness are both silent. Both demand to be heard, and each emotion is compelling, teaching us that life is what we make of it daily. The challenge for all of us is to learn how to celebrate the simple joys of those around us, to be honest, and authentic on those sad days, and to face the challenges that change our lives head-on. This is the fate of humankind — every one of us. I was content and would have been even if I hadn't been chosen for that game. I didn't need to brag about it to let everyone know how proud I was.

I was content simply because I had discovered how to have fun while doing what I loved most in the world. I was enjoying the journey regardless of the outcome.

When the All-Star voting period came, my teammates and coaches campaigned on my behalf, recognizing the dedication and talent I brought to the team. Seeing me through their eyes would be something I would never forget. By then, I felt I didn't need anyone's approval to know what I was doing was right yet hearing them talk about my accomplishments made me so proud. I had contributed something good to the lives of others. They had seen me strive to the point of exhaustion to be better every day, and they felt the lift from my words of encouragement that had helped them on difficult days. They both listened to my words and followed my advice.

Oh, what a feeling! Even today, it's impossible for me to explain how it felt to know that I had given back a little bit of all the good that had been given to me.

Finally, the day came when the All-Star selections were announced, and my teammates, coaches, family, and friends gathered to join me. I couldn't help but be nervous about the outcome. Although I was happy with my life, I couldn't deny how great it would be to have the opportunity to showcase my ability on the biggest stage of the sport I loved so much.

Just like that day when the young boys gathered around the coach to hear the names of the ones selected for Willow Creek, my friends, teammates, and family were gathered around to listen to the name of the All-Stars.

The moment they called my name, and I opened my eyes to see the people most important to me in the world jumping and screaming, celebrating what I had accomplished, time stopped, and the earth ceased spinning, locking me in the glorious moment. I felt them hug, congratulate, and shake me — but time had ceased to exist. Overcome with emotion, I felt my eyes stinging as the tears built up and spilled out. I wasn't aware of anything until my father hooked me by the shoulders and made me look him in the eye, bringing me back to this time and space. Next to him was my mother, crying with happiness and smiling like I had never seen her before.

All-Star Aspirations

"I feel so proud of you, son," my father said, holding me tightly. I know, wherever he is, Mr. Davis feels it too."

It was one of those hugs that felt like they were putting all the pieces of my body back together. Until that moment, I had been nothing more than a broken toy, scattered and shattered pieces, and my dad's embrace had fixed me.

Then I felt it. I saw my father cry for the first time, and I felt his tears on my shoulder as he patted my back. He kept repeating how proud they were of me. I had now come to realize that they always worked tirelessly because they knew that one way or another, I was going to get as much as I could from the game and go as far as my ability would take me. My work ethic came from my parents and their parents before them. Hard work was a mindset, my father would always say, "sometimes you have to do, what you have to do for as long as you have to do it!" I never really understood those words until this moment!

Over the course of my career, I had come to understand that baseball wasn't anything more than the vehicle that would take me wherever I wanted. As I prepared for my upcoming All-Star weekend, my wife Karyn was making sure that the family knew our itinerary and event schedule. She was so much more organized than I ever could be. She had always been a highly organized student since our days at USC. In our first Roman history class, when I asked to see her notes, I knew that day that Karyn was the person I wanted to share the ride with. Not sure she was ever a big baseball fan, but she at least pretended to enjoy her days at the ballparks even if it meant going to the smallest towns and parks across the country. After watching the homerun derby, one of the big events at the MLB All-star game, reporters asking questions, fans asking for autographs, out of the corner of my eye, I saw Karyn in the background, standing apart from the crowd, letting my parents be at the center of my joy. Karyn, the woman I loved, had become the true centerpiece of my life. My best friend. She was smiling at me as if waiting for her moment to embrace me, her eyes full of pride. Karyn had a way of making me feel like the luckiest man alive. She had become that person with whom I wanted to share everything: the good and the bad, the ordinary and the special. Absolutely everything, just with her.

Karyn and I met during our junior year at USC in an Italian History class. It was as if fate had brought us together. Karyn was not only incredibly intelligent but also kind-hearted and loving. We bonded over shared interests, spending time together studying and getting to know each other. Our relationship grew over the years, and eventually, we knew we were meant to be together. We married in Willow Creek, our hometown, and purchased a home there to start our life together.

Karyn had a passion for crafts and art, particularly drawing and designing women's clothing. Her creativity and talent always amazed me. She would spend hours sketching her designs, bringing them to life on paper. Her passion inspired me and reminded me of the importance of pursuing one's dreams.

Despite the demands of my baseball career, Karyn remained a constant pillar of support. While she finished her degree at USC, she would visit me during the season, understanding the commitment I had to my craft. Karyn had a calming presence and a nurturing nature. She knew how to give me the space I needed to focus on my career while also keeping me grounded as a couple. Her love and understanding meant the world to me.

One of the things I loved most about Karyn was her calm and relaxed demeanor. She had a way of putting things into perspective and reminding me of what truly mattered in life. Whenever I faced challenges or setbacks, she was there to listen, to offer words of encouragement, and to remind me of my own strength. With her by my side, I felt invincible.

Our journey together had been filled with memorable moments. From our first meeting at USC to the day we exchanged vows, Karyn had been there every step of the way. We had created a life together, built on love, trust, and unwavering support.

As I stood there, basking in the glory of my achievements, I knew that none of it would have been possible without Karyn. She had become my rock, my anchor in the storm. Her belief in me had never wavered, even during the toughest times. She was the person I wanted to share every success and failure with, the person who made every moment more meaningful.

At that moment, I recalled a conversation with Mr. Davis that had stayed with me. We had sat on his porch one evening, talking about life and love. He had said, "There will come a time when you meet someone who stands out from the crowd, someone with whom you can communicate without words." I finally understood his words. Karyn was that person for me—the one who understood.

"I love you," she whispered, enunciating those words so I could read her lips from across the field. At that point, I was confident that this achievement and all those that followed would be a personal triumph and a tribute to the support and guidance I had received from Mr. Davis, my friends, my parents, my teammates, my coaches, and her. The dream of that lonely, uncoordinated kid had become the dream of the people around me.

When the day finally came to take the field for the All-Star Game, I felt a mixture of excitement, nerves, and gratitude. I knew that I was playing not only for myself but for everyone who believed in me and helped me along the way. With the lessons of my past firmly in mind, I played with heart and determination.

In the end, although the loss of the All-Star Game was just another game in the grand scheme of things, the experience was a turning point for me. It solidified my faith in my abilities and the power of hard work, humility, and perseverance. When I returned to the Giants, I carried with me a renewed determination to continue growing as a player and person, both on and off the field. No matter what, I firmly intended to give back to the world the opportunities and love I had received over the years.

CHAPTER 12

Legacy and Lessons

As the years passed, my career in the major leagues continued to flourish. I had transformed into the player I would have admired when I was a kid, known not only for my skill on the field but also recognized for my humility, sportsmanship, and dedication to the game.

As I entered the twilight of my career, I began to think about the legacy I would leave behind. I knew that my accomplishments on the field were just one part of my story. The impact I had made on the lives of others, both within the world of baseball and beyond, was equally important. I decided to give back to the community that had supported me since my sandlot days.

I wanted to be "George Davis" to someone, paying forward his kindness. I knew I couldn't help every child fulfill his or her dream; that goal was too big. But I could start with small gestures, one by one, just like Mr. Davis did for me. In that way, my influence could grow and spread from me to them and, hopefully, from them to others. One good deed at a time could touch hundreds or thousands of people.

The idea of helping to foster a community where people would support each other was always top of mind. Over the years, I learned that a tiny gesture could unleash a wave of kindness with ripple effects that extend far and wide. If I planted the seed and watered it enough, others could reap the fruits and continue my legacy by caring for the people, places, and treasures they had been given.

There were times when I wondered if my idea was too naive. Expecting what I started to be adopted and preserved by others sometimes seemed grandiose and other times insufficient. But inside me, something urged me forward and assured me that my words wouldn't be ignored. Over time, I became convinced that if I managed to help at least one person — just one — it would somehow be worth the effort.

My plan started by returning to my beloved Willow Creek, where it all began. I traveled there during the off-season and organized a baseball clinic for the local kids, hoping to inspire the next generation of players and share the lessons I learned through my journey. I named the clinic "Davis-Thompson Baseball Camp" to ensure that the laughing old man who poured into my life that fantastic summer (and beyond) was never to be forgotten. He did what many others didn't: he looked beyond my awkward, uncoordinated body and saw the heart of a player ripe and ready to be cultivated. The least I could do was offer that same opportunity to others.

As I watched the young players at the clinic, I couldn't help but see myself.

Some were those natural athletes I always wished I was. Some were not. I knew each had a unique journey ahead of them, full of challenges, triumphs, and lessons to learn. And I only hoped that, by sharing my experiences and knowledge, I could provide them with the guidance and support that had long ago been crucial to my success.

I also established a scholarship fund. I will never forget the joy and relief the scholarship that allowed me to start my career brought to my parents. Deep inside, something asked me to spare other children that feeling of helplessness that I experienced inside me during my youth.

I knew that it was frankly impossible to help all those parents who, like mine, were giving everything to their children to have the opportunity to fulfill their dreams. And yet, with the remote possibility of knowing that a kid could live the happiness that I was able to experience, my work would not have been in vain. I would provide financial assistance for promising young athletes, ensuring they only worry about being their best selves daily.

That's not the only thing I thought about that winter, though. It was clear that I had to help those children who, like me, were just waiting for someone to give them a chance to show who they were. It was even more apparent that I wanted to be as present as possible in my children's lives. I wanted to be the one to teach them how to hold a bat, throw the ball, and to run the bases. I taught them the importance of footwork and finding the key to their moves in detail. I wanted to share with them everything Mr. Davis taught me that summer and everything I had learned throughout my career.

At Willow Creek, I realized I wanted to return to that old sandlot to play with my sons, George, and David. I wanted them to have a father that I didn't have growing up. If my legacy was scholarship, the clinic, and all the good I could do, they would be its very ambassadors. Although, at that time, they were still too young for all of that.

Years after that winter, I would stand on the field for my last game as a Major League player. I remember that day as if it were yesterday. When I put my feet on the field, it was the first time nerves didn't run through my body. I remember that the feeling of calmness and gratitude was the only thing in me. I spent so many years doing what I loved most in the world. Although it was ending, I could only wait impatiently to find out what the next stage of my life would bring.

That afternoon, the field was full of people ready to say goodbye to my career with me. Most of them I did not know, but I looked at them with gratitude, thankful for their support and for never losing faith in me. The friends who gathered for my last game were even more important to me that afternoon. Some had been by my side from the beginning, and others I met along the way. And yet, I knew they had been and would be there through the obstacles I had overcome and those I had yet to beat. The love for the country's national pastime had brought us together and molded us into the people we became.

But if anyone stood out in that vast crowd, it was my family. My parents—who unfortunately could no longer be there—were with me in my heart. Mr. Davis, who I felt like so many times before, resting his hand on my shoulder as if he were still there with me. And my wife and sons.

That woman who started out as the best friend I could ever wish for ended up being the person to share my life with forever. Over the years, we learned to understand each other, to give each other our space, and to love each other more and better every day. Karyn was my co-pilot, the person with whom I wanted to share all the journeys life had in store for us. She gave me my two greatest triumphs: George and David, our kids.

Honestly, until I saw my firstborn son's face, I thought my baseball achievements would be the greatest thing I had done in my life. But I was just a fool. Those boys were what I lived up for and hearing them cheering me on that afternoon with the love of my life by their side was all I needed. Doesn't matter where we are; I would be able to hear them above the crowd every time as if the world kept silent so I could listen to them.

I had to be grateful for many things in my life. But that day, what I felt most thankful for was them. I had become the player of my dreams and a man my kids could look to as they grew up. I had become the husband and the father I dreamt of, one they could go to when in need, somebody trustworthy and supportive. My house was full of the people I wanted to spend my life with now.

Baseball has given me the life I could only dream of as a child. Still, my family gave me the life I never thought I needed. They were my pride. I was sure the years ahead would have nothing to envy in my professional career just because wherever life led me, they would be by my side.

That afternoon, I finally understood my parents and Mr. Davis when they spoke about parenting. I would do anything for my sons. I would do anything for my beloved Karyn. I would set the world on fire if that was what it took to keep them safe. Even if those who had once been the pillars of my life weren't there anymore, I would keep their memories safe in my heart and share every story I had of them with my sons.

The people on my journey not only changed my life from beginning to end, but they also changed the lives of those around me and those who came after. The uncoordinated kid of Willow Creek's sandlot had become a man who put family first above everything else. That clumsy, unathletic boy I once was would always be by my side, reminding me that no matter how arduous the journey is—no matter how many stops you must make—no matter if you have to change the route or even the destination, if you bring the right people with you and have fun, you'll find happiness anyway.

As I walked off the field for the last time, I knew my journey in baseball was far from over. I would continue to share my passion for the game with others, passing on the lessons I had learned and the love of the sport that had fueled my journey from the sandlot to the major leagues.

Jack Thompson's legacy would live on in the record books and the hearts and minds of those I had inspired along the way. From the dusty sandlot in Willow Creek to the bright lights of the major leagues, my story was a testament to the power of hard work, perseverance, and the enduring magic of the great game, America's National Pastime Baseball!.

CHAPTER 13

Memories and Reminiscences

A few weeks after my last game, Karyn, and the boys, and I moved back to Willow Creek so they could grow up as I did: free and happy. I wanted my kids to have many cheerful moments as I had in my youth — to play at the old sandlot, run on the streets, and go on adventures with their friends. None of those simple joys were possible in a big city. So, after considering it, we moved to the old town where everything started for me.

The years passed, and our kids grew up as fast as the clinic I started. The clinic became more popular, and we expanded the project to help as many children as possible who, like me, needed someone who believed in them. The scholarship fund helped two kids fulfill their dreams and play at the college level every year.

Helping others became the center of my life. I wanted to give back all the good I had received and more. Something within me said that inspiring children was as much an accomplishment as my major league career. I knew it would be my life's work to ensure each felt listened to, understood, and inspired to reach their dreams. I especially enjoyed talking to those kids who doubted themselves. My message to kids like this stayed the same: it's not how you start; it will always be how you finish that matters. Your passion and hard work will always decide how you find your way in the world.

I told them my stories and listened to theirs just as Mr. Davis and I had done all those years ago. Each had something in common with me: a passion for the incredible world of sports. Some played football, others basketball, and a few hockey, but most loved baseball as much as I did. All those kids had extraordinary lives ahead of them, and they gave their best with every step they took. Some realized the dream and became professional players, while others found their paths elsewhere. They lived humbly and were grateful for their time in the clinic. As adults, many of them returned to the clinics and universities to tell their stories as they tried to influence other kids with their experiences and lessons. It didn't matter that some did not go all the way; what mattered was that they knew they had the choice. Nothing was impossible for them.

As I saw my ambitious project grow, my heart filled with pride. The lessons of Mr. Davis were passed down to a new generation of hopefuls with stars in their eyes. His words will never be forgotten as those kids grew into adults and taught his wisdom to their children. His message of determination, hard work, and passion will stay alive forever in the minds of these new generations. Within each kid, part of him lived, making this a better world. He had become immortal, living on in the hearts of the lives we touched.

Today, I'm older than Mr. Davis was when I first met him. I became the one sitting on a rickety wooden bench near the edge of the field, hair graying, body a little less limber with each passing year. It was my turn to look out over the field while watching my grandchildren play. As they ran, threw, and caught the balls, calling to each other, I understood what he saw long ago.

Though I was eternally grateful to him for all he taught me, one question lingered, begging to be answered: why? Why had he given so much of his time and effort to help me? Why was he even there that day, watching me play? Why me?

I vividly remember one summer evening, just before heading off to my first semester in college when I could no longer wait, I asked him why he was spending the days with me, helping me improve my baseball skills. He talked about something called the butterfly effect, a concept that fascinated and intrigued him. He explained that the butterfly effect suggested that even the smallest of actions could have profound and far-reaching consequences — like a butterfly flapping its wings in one part of the world resulting in a blustery hurricane someplace else.

His eyes filled with a mixture of sadness and gratitude as he revealed a truth that touched my soul. "Jack," he began, his voice soft and tinged with emotion, "I may have been teaching you about baseball, but in many ways, you were teaching me about life. You see, I lost my only child, my son, many years ago. And in you, I found a kindred spirit, a son I never knew I needed. The time we spent together, the bond we formed, filled a void in my heart that I thought could never be filled."

Tears welled in my eyes as I listened to his words. I had never imagined that our connection ran so deep, that I had become a source of healing for him, just as he had been for me. It was a beautiful revelation, a testament to the power of human connection and the ways in which our lives intertwine, shaping and transforming us.

From that moment forward, our bond grew even stronger. Mr. Davis became more than a mentor; he became a cherished member of my family. We shared countless memories and conversations, always knowing that our connection was something truly special.

As I continued my journey in baseball and beyond, I carried his wisdom, his love, and his spirit with me. I made it my mission to pass on the lessons I had learned, not just on the field, but about life itself. And as I watched the ripple effect of his influence spread through the generations, I knew that his legacy would continue to touch lives long after we were both gone.

The butterfly effect, it seemed, was not just a theory—it was a tangible reality. The small actions, the insignificant moments, carried the power to shape destinies and touch souls. And in the interconnected web of our lives, we found purpose, meaning, and the profound impact we could have on each other.

As I gazed out at the field, watching my grandchildren play, I felt an overwhelming sense of gratitude. Gratitude for the lessons, the love, and the immeasurable impact of one man's kindness. Mr. Davis had given me more than just baseball skills; he had given me the true meaning of family, a true chance at belonging to something bigger than myself.

And as I embraced my role as a father and grandfather, passing on the legacy of love and the game, I knew that the butterfly effect would continue its dance, carrying us all forward, weaving our lives together in ways we could never fully comprehend. The circle of life, of love, and of baseball, would forever be intertwined, leaving a legacy that transcended time and touched the hearts of generations to come.

As I grew older, his lessons became more apparent in my head, and his sad smiles more vivid. That man changed not only my life but my whole family. He taught me about baseball, life, youth, and parenting. It is hard to believe that he changed so much about my future in such an abbreviated time. But he just needed one summer to turn my life upside down.

When I saw my sons and their kids, I could not help wondering what Mr. Davis felt every time I stepped on the field. He arrived at that same sandlot and saw me there waiting for him with eager eyes and a willing heart. I wondered how he could extend his hand to help me when he was the one who needed help. I wondered how he showed me such love when his heart was breaking — the father without a son.

Those afternoons we spent together were as much for him as they were for me. The memory of everything we had lived together was all he had left. His laughter expresses his love of baseball, and his melancholy eyes reflect the horrible truth that he and his son had no more summers to live together.

I had never forgotten that afternoon when he opened up and told me the saddest of his stories. I was still incredibly young then, and I could only think that I hoped I would never have to go through something like that. Some dads mourn the loss of their sons, so internally, the grief devours them. But Mr. Davis chose to channel his grief by pouring it into my life, teaching me baseball. He found solace in sharing his knowledge and passion for the sport, using it as a conduit for healing and connection. As we spent countless hours on the field, his grief transformed into a profound sense of purpose, as if his son's memory lived on through our shared love for the game. Mr. Davis's dedication to me went beyond teaching the technical aspects of baseball. He became a mentor, a confidant, and a source of unwavering support. Through our interactions, I could sense that he found comfort in watching my growth and witnessing the potential that his son could have had. In his eyes, my successes became a testament to his son's spirit, a way to honor his memory by fostering my dreams and aspirations.

The bond we formed transcended the boundaries of coach and player; it was a connection forged by shared pain, resilience, and the determination to transform grief into something meaningful. Mr. Davis's choice to channel his grief into guiding me reflected his strength and a testament to the power of finding purpose despite his crushing heartbreak. Through his selfless acts, he taught me invaluable life lessons that extended far beyond the diamond. He taught me the importance of resilience, compassion, and the transformative power of pouring oneself into the lives of others. In honoring his son's memory, Mr. Davis helped me become a better baseball player and inspired me to embrace life's challenges with courage and grace.

"Every moment, Jack — every moment with the people you love is a priceless treasure. Make the most of every second you have with them, and don't let time slip away from you. Sometimes, I'd like to go back and watch my son sleep peacefully in his bed, surrounded by baseball posters. I wish I could see him just once more, stumble out of bed on Sunday mornings, and go out to play on the porch."

I remember the tears that backed up behind his eyes and occasionally spilled out. I remember him looking away so that I would see him wiping them away. I remember that sad smile that never left him and the voice broken by the years of grief.

"If you ever have children, Jack, remember that they will become your reason for living. Your aspirations and dreams for them will become meaningless if their safety is threatened. You are responsible for making them future leaders, and that one, young man, will be the most difficult challenge you will ever face. Yet, it will be the most rewarding."

That old man really knew what he was saying. I never loved baseball more than when I started to instruct my sons in the backyard. I never felt as much for my team as I felt for my sons'. They made every step on my way look tiny compared to the ones they made.

Seeing my sons enjoy baseball with me since they were little, their first summer in the sandlot, their first game in the junior league, their first day of high school, and their first day of college eclipsed any successes I experienced on the field. Even though neither wanted to follow my path and become professional players, baseball continued to be the link that united our family. No matter how far away they were as adults, we would get together every year to watch the All-Star game and try to go to a stadium at least once a year to share our passion as a family.

Then fortune smiled on me when my older grandson decided that he wanted to follow in my footsteps. There are no words to explain what I felt every time he came to our home, asking me to tell him the stories of my youth, begging for a few minutes outside to toss the ball. I lacked the words to describe the light in his eyes when he played at the old sandlot, knowing it was the place where I was reborn. A fierce will was living inside of him, a force capable of taking him wherever he wanted.

I will never forget his first game at the big-league level. Throughout my life, I have tried to be that pillar on which the people around me could lean. I always wanted to be there to show my support, answer questions, and provide a healthy dose of inspiration. But that afternoon, the first time I watched as my grandson ran out onto the field, I felt my legs failing me. My hands were shaking as they never had before, and my eyes immediately filled with tears. Unlike my father, I had been lucky enough to live long enough to know my grandchildren and participate in their lives. I got the blessing of enjoying their company and hearing their laughter. But I never thought seeing them succeed in the big leagues would be possible. I always worried that would be the only dream I could never fulfill. Yet, that afternoon and those that followed, I saw my first grandchild delight the fans in a Major League stadium.

My heart swelled with pride when the middle grandson announced that he wanted to work at the Willow Creek clinic to help the children there. He decided this was the way he wanted to continue my legacy — in a life of service helping others. And so, he did. Maybe it wasn't the dream he had as a child, but he caught the vision I shared by my example. Today, he spends his life helping kids worldwide enjoy the sport of baseball.

The rest of my grandchildren are still trying to discover their path in life. The blessing of youth is that they still have time to unearth their destinies. As they grow and share their plans, dreams, and fears with us, Karyn and I realize that this life was the best we could have crafted. Getting together every summer with our children and grandchildren to eat on the porch while laughing at the stories the little ones tell us is and always will be the most incredible gift life could have given us.

Now I'm older. I hope and pray that I am wiser. I am sure that everything I have lived through, the ups and downs, the bumps and surprises, the stops, the starts, the changes, the highs and lows along the way, and everything that life has put in front of me have been a part of the formula that brings me to this moment. After a life full of challenges and victories, I have come to realize that no award or success of my own will ever compare to the pride that comes from being able to share time with the people you love most in this world and see them develop into the best version of themselves. At my age, I have finally learned that the most essential thing in this life is the beautiful collection of people we choose to walk the path toward our dreams with.

Finally, it doesn't matter where you come from or where you go if the people beside you to experience life with you are the right ones. Those people will be the ones who will be there for the greatest of your defeats. They will be the reason for your laughter and the driving force behind your greatest triumphs. Finding someplace to call home and having someone to come home to is all that truly matters. We build our lives together as our paths converge to happiness. One of the most difficult challenges you will ever face is learning to focus on the essential elements of life and minimizing the things that don't matter.

Knowing what I know now, if I could do it all again, I would walk the same path again and again—and again and again—if I were assured that it would always lead to this moment… to these people I call my family, my friends.

I was just a child back then when it all started. The miracle is in the wonder that the uncoordinated lonely child from Willow Creek became the player, husband, father, and mentor I am.

I am so thankful George Davis taught me to never dream small or quietly. "Dream big and dream loudly, speak and live your dreams into existence young man, your dreams are yours to carry for as long as you choose to carry them!"

Made in United States
Cleveland, OH
03 April 2025